KISSING

"Each girl names a boyfriend," Debby said. "The way you eliminate a player from the game is by kissing her boyfriend. The winner is the girl whose boyfriend holds out the longest."

"But you have to kiss them in public," said Amanda.

"And you can't tell your boyfriends about the game," added Linda.

"What a stupid game," said Tasha, giggling.

"I don't blame you for not liking it." Debby looked at her coolly. "It'd be too easy to kiss Billy."

18 Pine St.

Dangerous Games

Written by
Stacie Johnson

Created by
WALTER DEAN MYERS

A Seth Godin Production

BANTAM BOOKS
NEW YORK · TORONTO · LONDON · SYDNEY · AUCKLAND

RL 5, age 10 and up

DANGEROUS GAMES
A Bantam Book / September 1993

Thanks to Susan Korman, Betsy Gould, Amy Berkower, Fran Lebowitz, Marva Martin, Michael Cader, Megan O'Connor, José Arroyo, Julie Maner, Kate Grossman, Ellen Kenny, Helene and Lucy Wood.

18 Pine St. is a trademark of Seth Godin Productions, Inc.

ISBN 0-553-56269-X

Published simultaneously in the United States and Canada

Bantam Books are published by Bantam Books, a division of Bantam Doubleday Dell Publishing Group, Inc. Its trademark, consisting of the words "Bantam Books" and the portrayal of a rooster, is Registered in U.S. Patent and Trademark Office and in other countries. Marca Registrada. Bantam Books, 1540 Broadway, New York, New York 10036.

PRINTED IN THE UNITED STATES OF AMERICA

OPM 0 9 8 7 6 5 4 3 2 1

For Leah

18 Pine St.

There is a card shop at 8 Pine Street, and a shop that sells sewing supplies at 10 Pine that's only open in the afternoons and on Saturdays if it doesn't rain. For some reason that no one seems to know or care about, there is no 12, 14, or 16 Pine. The name of the pizzeria at 18 Pine Street was Antonio's before Mr. and Mrs. Harris took it over. Mr. Harris removed Antonio's sign and just put up a sign announcing the address. By the time he got around to thinking of a name for the place, everybody was calling it 18 Pine.

The Crew at 18 Pine St.

Sarah Gordon is the heart and soul of the group. Sarah's pretty, with a great smile and a warm, caring attitude that makes her a terrific friend. Sarah's the reason that everyone shows up at 18 Pine St.

Tasha Gordon, tall, sexy, and smart, is Sarah's cousin. Since her parents died four years ago, Tasha has moved from relative to relative. Now she's living with Sarah and her family—maybe for good.

Cindy Phillips is Sarah's best friend. Cindy is petite, with dark, radiant skin and a cute nose. She wears her black hair in braids. Cindy's been Sarah's neighbor and friend since she moved from Jamaica when she was three.

Kwame Brown's only a sophomore, but that doesn't stop him from being part of the crew. Kwame's got a flattop haircut and mischievous smile. As the smartest kid in the group, he's the one Jennifer turns to for help with her homework.

Jennifer Wilson is the poor little rich girl. Her parents are divorced, and all the charge cards and clothes in the world can't make up for it. Jennifer's tall and thin, with cocoa-colored skin and a body that's made for all those designer clothes she wears.

April Winter has been to ten schools in the last ten years—and she hopes she's at Murphy to stay. Her energy, blond hair, and offbeat personality make her a standout at school.

José Melendez seems to be everyone's friend. Quiet and unassuming, José is always happy to help out with a homework assignment or project.

And there's Dave Hunter, Brian Wu, and the rest of the gang. You'll meet them all in the halls of Murphy High and after school for a pizza at 18 Pine St.

18 PINE

One

"You should have seen his face!" said Kwame Brown, gasping for breath. He took off his black-framed glasses, wiped his eyes with his sleeve, and started laughing again.

Kwame sat with his friends at their favorite pizzeria, 18 Pine St., in the wide back booth they considered their own. Kwame told them he had seen Mr. Schlesinger, the assistant principal at Murphy High, slip and fall in front of the school earlier that November afternoon.

"I was in math class, and I just happened to be looking out the window, and there he was, cutting across the muddy patch near the bike rack," said Kwame. "One minute he was tiptoeing through the mud, then he slipped, ran in place for a few seconds, and wound up sprawled on his back with this look on his face!" Kwame tilted his glasses, looked at the ceiling, and mimicked the assistant principal's dazed expression.

His friends roared.

"Man, I'd give anything to see him fall on his butt like that," said Billy Turner. "He's always giving me a hard time."

"You deserve it," said Tasha Gordon, giving him a playful poke with her elbow.

Billy Turner looked at Tasha's cousin, Sarah. "See how your cousin treats me?"

Sarah Gordon giggled. When Tasha and Billy were getting along, the two juniors at Murphy High seemed like the ideal couple. Earlier this year Tasha had come to Madison to live with Sarah's family, some time after an accident claimed the lives of her own parents. Despite the tragedy, Tasha was outgoing and self-assured. Her skin was the color of dark honey, and her hair fell down to her shoulder blades in polished black waves. That afternoon she wore a bright red paisley blouse with pearl buttons, and a pair of carefully torn blue jeans.

Billy sat beside her, his equipment bag on the table. He was handsome and stocky, with a broad face and intense, wide-set eyes. He kept his hair very short, like the rest of the Murphy High football team. As captain of the team, he was well known for his speed and strength, but Tasha's presence on the girls' basketball team brought her equal respect. The two of them had immediately been drawn to one another.

Many people thought Sarah was the exact opposite of Tasha. While Tasha dazzled the boys, Sarah charmed them with her quiet, even-tempered personal-

2

ity. She didn't dare copy her cousin's reckless flair for fashion. Her style was more like beige pants and a blue cable-knit sweater. Her hair was short and permed in soft waves.

"What a day," said Billy, yawning loudly. He pulled his duffel bag closer and rested his head on it.

Tasha nudged him before he got too comfortable. "Get off the table, Billy," she said, "that's rude."

"I don't hear anybody complaining," Billy murmured, his voice muffled by the bag. Tasha pushed him again, but he didn't budge.

"You know what would put me in a great mood?" said Kwame. "A slice of turkey pizza."

"Turkey pizza!" said Steve Adams, wrinkling his nose and clutching his throat.

"Why not?" said Kwame. "Billy loves pepperoni pizza; Tasha loves veggie pizza. Why not turkey pizza?"

"You'll eat anything, Kwame!" said Cindy Phillips. "But turkey pizza? People don't want to eat turkey anything until Thanksgiving."

"I'd try a slice," said Sarah. She was almost back to her normal weight after a terrible car accident that had put her in a coma. She still suffered headaches and dizziness, but the doctors had told her that was normal. What didn't seem normal was how hungry she'd been since the accident. The veggie pizza slice she'd ordered that afternoon had disappeared in a hurry—including the crust.

Mr. Harris seemed to have read her mind. The

3

owner of the pizzeria suddenly appeared at their table with a thick brownie on a plate. He set it down in front of Sarah and motioned for her to eat.

"Thanks, Mr. Harris, but I shouldn't have anything else," said Sarah.

"Please, Sarah, you'll hurt my feelings," said Mr. Harris. "Besides, you're still skin and bones."

Sarah opened her mouth to object, but Mr. Harris was already distracted.

"Look at this," he said, pointing to the wall above their booth. "It's disgusting, all the graffiti I got here. Who writes these things?" He squinted at a phrase on the wall. "'For a good time, call K.C.' Sheesh! This week, I'm buying a roller and some paint and redoing this whole wall."

"Let me copy that girl's number down before you start," Billy joked. Tasha elbowed him again.

"If I paint it blue, you won't see the graffiti as much," said Mr. Harris, almost to himself.

"Blue will make the place much darker, especially with these dark brown booths," said Tasha, who had a good eye for design.

"I could always hang some pictures to liven up the place," said Mr. Harris. "Maybe some nice mountain scenes, or some cowboys."

"Don't forget to put up one of Charlie Black," said Kwame.

"Who?" said Mr. Harris.

Kwame's friends looked at him as well.

"Charlie Black, the great black rodeo champion,"

4

Kwame explained.

"I never heard of a black cowboy," said Mr. Harris.

"There were lots of them. The trouble is nobody's heard of them," said Kwame.

"Uh-oh, Kwame's gettin' started," said Billy. They laughed.

"Straight up," said Kwame, looking at his friend. "I bet you could tell me the name of twenty black football heroes, but you can't tell me who Charles Drew was."

"I was sick that day," Billy mumbled.

"Charles Drew was a black doctor who discovered blood plasma," said Mr. Harris. He grinned when he noticed Kwame's look of surprise. "He's in my stamp collection. You want me to put his picture on the wall?"

"Not just him," said Kwame eagerly. "Other little-known black heroes."

"I don't know...." said Mr. Harris.

"I think we should get pictures of ourselves. We're the ones who hang out back here," said Cindy.

"Yeah," said Billy, "Some of us are little-known black heroes!"

"I'll think about it," said Mr. Harris. He saw some customers near the cash register and hurried back to his counter. "Tell you what," he called back, "bring in some pictures. If I like them, I'll put them up."

"I'm going to take him up on it," said Kwame determinedly.

"Don't get too excited," Steve warned. "Remember when he wanted us to come up with a name for his all-meat pizza? He ended up naming it after his dog!"

"This is different," said Kwame, jotting down names on the cover of his notebook.

Cindy pointed to the brownie on Sarah's plate. "Go ahead and eat it," she whispered. "I know you want to."

Cindy and Sarah had been best friends ever since Cindy's family had moved to Madison from Jamaica. The two had grown up together, sharing toys, adventures and secrets. Now that Tasha lived at Sarah's ho   Cindy and Sarah didn't get together as often as the   d to. But they still had a knack for reading each o   's minds.

"W   lf?" asked Sarah.

"Wha   friends for?" Cindy grinned as she picked up a fork.

Steve ran   over his unruly red hair. "I hate to brag," he bega   ropped three more cans of tuna in the hom   day. Thank you very much." He leaned b   ooth. The holiday canned food drive was a   at Murphy High School. Each class competed to   ng in the most donations before the vacation.

"Way to go, Steve. It looks like the j   ors are holding their lead," Tasha said. "I think we're   ing to beat the seniors this year."

"The seniors always win," said Billy, still slouched over his duffel bag.

"Not this time, Billy," said Tasha. "Our class has more school spirit than theirs does." She tapped him

6

on the head with her empty soda cup on her way to get a refill.

As Billy closed his eyes and shifted his body to get more comfortable, Sarah's eye fell on his equipment bag, which was partway open. Wedged between a pair of sweat socks and Billy's scuffed football shoes, she noticed a shiny black shape. She stared at it until she recognized what it was. It couldn't be, she thought. It looked like the handle of a gun. A chill raced up her back.

Cindy saw the look in Sarah's eyes and followed her gaze. She carefully poked a finger into the zippered opening to get a better view. When she saw what had frightened Sarah, she inhaled sharply.

"What's up?" said Kwame, looking at them. "You look like you've seen a ghost."

"Or my French grade," said Steve with a chuckle.

Sarah took a pen and paper from her book bag and wrote, "Billy has a gun in his bag." She showed it to Kwame and Steve.

"No way," Steve mouthed, leaning over to take a look for himself.

Tasha came back and noticed how quiet her friends were. She saw the note on the table before she sat down. Without hesitating, she reached into the duffel bag. The movement jostled Billy, who opened his eyes and saw Tasha's arm two inches away.

"What are you doing?" he said, grabbing for her arm.

Tasha had pulled the gun out and dangled it by the

handle. "What are you carrying this for?" she demanded.

"It's a squirt gun!" said Kwame. The plastic toy looked a lot less threatening now that it was out of the bag.

Sarah felt her face get warm as Steve gave her an "I told you so" look.

"Give me that!" Billy growled. He stood up to grab it from Tasha's hand, but she stepped away from the booth.

"Aren't you a little old to be fooling with toys?" said Tasha playfully. She squeezed the trigger and a stream of water shot onto the "M" emblazoned on Billy's jacket.

"Don't do that," Billy warned. He extended his hand and waited for Tasha to give him the water gun.

Tasha dropped the gun into his hand, and Billy put it back into his bag.

"Who taught you to go through people's things?" he asked indignantly. "If you want to see something, just ask."

"Well, I'm sorry, but you scared my friends," said Tasha. She put her hand on Sarah's shoulder. "In case you forgot, my cousin is recovering from a bad accident, and the last thing she needs is a shock."

Billy's eye fell on the note Sarah had written. "You all thought I had a real gun?" he said in disbelief.

"It looked real," said Sarah defensively. "You read about gangs and violence, and you never know who's involved."

"Yeah, but *me*?" said Billy.

Cindy shrugged. "You never know, Billy. We were concerned."

"I know what it's like to be accused of something you didn't do," said Steve, shooting Cindy a meaningful look. Earlier that month, Cindy had accused Steve of attacking his girlfriend, April Winter. It wasn't true, and Cindy had apologized, but Steve was still sensitive about the incident.

"Well, it's better to be safe, Steve," said Cindy, her voice beginning to rise. "I know you didn't hurt April, but..."

"Whoa, let's not start that again," said Kwame quickly. He looked at Billy. "You still haven't told us why you're packing a water gun."

"I'll tell you when Dave shows up," Billy promised.

Dave Hunter was Sarah's boyfriend. He was a likable junior who would have been popular even if he hadn't been one of the stars of the basketball team. That afternoon he had promised to stop by the pizzeria to take Sarah home.

"We can tell Dave later," said Tasha.

Billy looked at each of his friends until he was sure he had everyone's undivided attention. "It's part of a game," he said mysteriously. "I read about it in *Jet* magazine. Anybody here ever heard of KAOS?"

Nobody had.

"It stands for 'Killing As Organized Sport,'" said Billy. "In KAOS each player has a water gun and the name of a person he has to 'kill,' If he kills his target—."

9

"The target's out of the game!" Steve interrupted. "Your victim has to give you the name of the guy he was after, and that's your next target. In my old school, we called it 'Assassin.'"

"You keep killing off your victims and getting the name of your next 'hit.' Soon there are just two players left: the guy you're after, and the guy who's after you!" said Billy. "Isn't that great?"

"What a dumb game," said Cindy. The Gordon cousins nodded.

"Too violent for you?" said Billy with a smirk.

"No, it's just dumb," said Tasha. "You go around shooting your victims until you're the only one left. What's the point?"

"The point is to have fun," said Steve.

"It's such a typical guy's game," said Tasha scornfully. "Killing off other players. Kwame doesn't like it, do you, Kwame?" Tasha flashed her eyes at him.

Kwame shrugged.

"I don't like the guns," said Sarah. "Couldn't you use something else?"

"They're water guns, not the real thing," Steve protested.

"That's how it starts," said Cindy. "Remember that story in the news about the boy who squirted a man with a water gun, and the man turned around and shot him with a real gun?"

"That's not going to happen here," said Steve. "You're overreacting."

Tasha touched Steve's arm. "Maybe it's hard for you

to understand, but our people are getting killed on the street every day. Killing is one thing we don't have to play at."

Billy groaned. "This ain't a black and white thing, Tasha," he said. "It's just a game we're going to play. You make it sound like World War Three!"

Tasha glared at Billy. "Look, I used to live in Oakland, California. There were gangs out there that a small city like Madison doesn't have. So excuse me if I'm a little more sensitive than you are."

Billy sighed loudly. He brightened when he saw Dave Hunter approaching their table. "We'll ask Dave what he thinks, okay?"

"What's up?" said Dave. He flashed a quick smile at them, and gently squeezed Sarah's shoulder before pulling out a chair from a nearby table.

"How was your practice?" asked Sarah.

"I was a killer, as usual," Dave replied.

The girls winced at his choice of words.

"Listen, I can't stay," he said, looking apologetically at Tasha and Sarah. "Still want a ride?"

"I do," said Sarah, getting up. "But Tasha is getting a ride with Billy."

"No, I think I'll go with you," said Tasha pointedly.

Billy shrugged as if he didn't care one way or the other.

"What did you want to ask me, Billy?" said Dave.

Billy took out the water pistol and explained KAOS to Dave. The basketball star's face lit up into a broad grin. "Sounds like fun. When do we start?"

Sarah sighed. Didn't Dave have any sense either?

Tasha stood up to put on her coat. Suddenly she felt a spurt of water land on her hair and trickle into her scalp. She whirled around and glared at Billy. He chuckled as he put the squirt gun back in the duffel bag.

"We're even," he said, pointing to the "M" on his jacket.

Two

When the cousins walked through the front door, they saw Sarah's parents in the living room. Mrs. Gordon was flipping through one of her law journals, and Mr. Gordon was reading his notes for a school board speech. Sarah could tell they'd been arguing by the way each one was coolly ignoring the other. On the coffee table lay two piles of travel brochures. The scene had become familiar over the past two weeks as the Gordons tried to plan a vacation. They each had very different ideas about the ideal trip and some heated discussions had developed.

"Hi, girls, how was school?" Mr. Gordon said, looking up from his papers.

"Fine," Sarah and Tasha called back before disappearing into the kitchen.

"You would think two intelligent grown-ups would be able to decide where to go on vacation," Sarah mumbled.

Tasha nodded. She lifted the lid from the pot on the stove and inhaled the aroma. "Mmm, beef stew."

"I thought you were trying to be a vegetarian!" Sarah teased.

"Smelling doesn't count," said Tasha, putting the lid back.

"I still think they should go skiing," said Sarah.

"That's because you're a daddy's girl," said Tasha, opening the refrigerator and pulling out a jug of cider. She poured two glasses and handed one to her cousin. "Your mom has the right idea," she said between sips. "Go to the Bahamas, walk by the ocean in the moonlight, soak up the sun, ride horses on the beach, go dancing at a little club. Find a hot-looking island man...."

"Whoa, cuz! That's *your* fantasy," said Sarah, laughing. "My parents would probably tour the old forts, sit on the beach the rest of the time, and come home with a sunburn. All I know is, my dad wants to try out those new Rossignol skis he's got. He keeps saying he'll be the terror of the slopes."

"That's doesn't sound very romantic," said Tasha.

"Says who? Imagine a private cabin, with a big fire and some warm cocoa—"

"And a hot-looking ski instructor," Tasha added.

"You have a one-track mind, Ms. Gordon," said Sarah.

"Yeah!" said Tasha loudly. Her enthusiasm surprised them both, and they burst into laughter.

"Nice to see somebody having a good time," Mrs.

14

Gordon said, entering the kitchen. Sarah smiled at her mother. She loved the way Mrs. Gordon dressed at home. The outfits she wore in court made her look like a no-nonsense lawyer. But in her sweatpants, long-sleeved T-shirt, and slippers, she looked relaxed and comfortable. Sarah watched as Mrs. Gordon picked up a wooden spoon and stirred the beef stew a few times, then lowered the flame under it.

"Still haven't decided about the vacation?" Sarah asked.

Mrs. Gordon shook her head. "Your father is so stubborn." She sighed. "He knows I can't ski as well as he can."

Sarah's mother left the kitchen and went upstairs. Moments later her father walked in. Mr. Gordon was the principal of Hamilton, the other high school in Madison.

"What are you kids up to?" he said. He walked over to the pot on the stove and lifted the lid. After stirring it a few times, he turned up the flame slightly, and the stew bubbled faster.

"We're just hanging out," Sarah told him.

"That's good," said Mr. Gordon distractedly. He looked at them both. "Did your mother say anything about the vacation when she was in here?"

The girls shook their heads.

"Just wondering," said Mr. Gordon. He winked at Tasha. "Your aunt is impossible! She knows I can't swim as well as she can."

"I don't know if I can take this much longer," said

Sarah after he left.

"I know exactly what you mean," Tasha agreed.

At dinner that evening, everyone raved about the stew. The vacation topic was carefully avoided. Halfway through the meal, the phone rang and Sarah and Tasha's grandmother, Miss Essie, stood up to answer it.

"Let the machine get it, Mother," said Mr. Gordon. He didn't like his meals interrupted by the phone.

"Can't," said Miss Essie. "It could be from New York City."

Sarah was proud that grandmother still pursued her acting career. Earlier that month Miss Essie had performed at a dinner theater in a nearby town. A producer who made commercials had seen her, and had promised to call her about a possible job. Sarah knew that it had been the producer on the phone when Miss Essie returned from the kitchen wearing a broad smile.

"That was the man from New York," she said, sitting down again. "I'm going to try out for a coffee commercial!"

"All right, Miss Essie!" Tasha called.

"Congratulations, Mother," said Mr. Gordon, beaming.

"Miss Essie's going to be on TV!" said Allison, Sarah's eleven-year-old sister.

"Wait now, it's just a tryout," Miss Essie warned. "I don't know if I'll get it. It's for a coffee called Mornin'."

"I know you will," said Tasha confidently. "You've

16

got the Mornin' Coffee Look."

Miss Essie pursed her lips disdainfully. "It's one of those acid-free coffees they sell to us old people. I tried it once, and it wasn't hittin' on nuthin'."

"If you don't like the coffee, why are you going to do the commercial?" Allison asked.

"Honey, that's why they call it acting!"

After dinner Sarah helped her mother load the dishwasher. She told her about the KAOS game Billy was starting. "It's so childish," she said.

Mrs. Gordon shrugged. "A group of girls in my high school used to play meaner games than that. They would pick a girl who was a little shy and pretend to be her friend. The girl was so happy to be popular, she would do anything the gang asked her to. One girl was told to bring cigarettes to school for her 'friends'. Then the gang reported her, and she was suspended for three days."

"That's terrible!" Sarah cried. She looked at her mother with concern. "Did...did that happen to you?"

Mrs. Gordon laughed. "I didn't have time for any of that."

"You were too busy studying, I suppose," said Sarah.

"No, chasing Brian Barron. He was the conductor in the marching band, and I was a majorette."

"Did you ever go out with him?" asked Sarah.

Mr. Gordon came in with a stack of dirty plates.

"I'll tell you all about it sometime," Mrs. Gordon replied with a wink.

Tasha had her bedroom door closed, but Sarah could hear her radio blasting a heavy beat through the walls. Sarah knocked on her cousin's door as she walked by, and the volume of the music went down a tiny fraction.

Sarah's room was unusually messy. Her bed was unmade and clothes hung from the open dresser drawers. The struggle to catch up with the mound of missed schoolwork after the accident hadn't left her much time to do anything else.

She dropped her books on the desk, then straightened up her room. When the room was spotless, she had no choice but to face her trigonometry problems. "Ugh," she groaned. She heard the phone ring, and then Allison yelling her name. Sarah ran out to the hallway, grateful for the distraction.

"Hi," said Dave. "What's up?"

"Trig," said Sarah.

"Same here. Want to come over and work on it together?"

Sarah chuckled. "I don't know. Do you remember what happened the last time?"

"Hey, that was a fluke," Dave protested. "It wasn't like we were making out all night. Can I help it if my mom came into the kitchen right then?"

"I was so embarrassed," said Sarah.

"You should have heard her talking when you left."

"She didn't!" cried Sarah.

"I'm just ragging on you," said Dave, laughing. He paused, and his voice turned serious. "What was up with you and your cousin in the car today? You both

18

looked mad."

"I guess Tasha was upset with Billy about that killing game," said Sarah. "It kind of bothered me, too."

"Tasha's too sensitive, and you're too nice," Dave commented. "Actually, I could use a game to get my mind off school," he said, almost to himself. "Anyway, if you can't come over, why don't I go over there?"

"Sure," said Sarah. "I'll see you in a little while." She hung up, then headed straight for the bathroom.

"Someone's coming over," Tasha sang out. She stood at the door of the bathroom, leaning against the door frame, and watched Sarah dab her mouth with a clear, strawberry-scented lip gloss.

"We're just going to study together in the den," said Sarah, not taking her eyes off the mirror.

"Uh-huh, sure," teased Tasha. "That's why you need lip gloss?"

"Do I detect a little jealousy?" said Sarah as she brushed past her cousin.

"Ha!" Tasha cried. "I could have any boy at Murphy"—she paused—"come over and help me with my homework."

"Except Dave," Sarah called back. "He's mine." Then she gathered her books and headed for the stairs.

18
PINE

Three

The Murphy High PA system crackled before the assistant principal's voice was heard in all the homerooms the next morning. "There will be a pep rally for the football team's final game of the season this afternoon at the gymnasium," Mr. Schlesinger intoned. "The entire Murphy High community will report to the gym at two o'clock. After the pep rally all students will return immediately to their final class." Students all over the school cheered. There had been rumors about a pep rally, but Mr. Schlesinger was notorious for canceling such events at the last minute.

When the teachers got the announcement to lead their classes to the gymnasium, Kwame asked to be excused to go to the rest room. Instead of going to the one near his social studies class, he went to the rest room by the cafeteria, where Billy Turner had told all KAOS players to meet. When Kwame arrived, he noticed with pride that he was the only sophomore who

21

had been invited to play. Kwame recognized most of the guys, including Dave Hunter, Steve Adams, Robert Thornton, Marc Halle, Jimmy Walls, and Tyler McPeak. There were a few others he didn't know. He nodded to Steve, who was the only white student.

Billy leaned against a sink. He was dressed in his football uniform. Jimmy Walls, a running back, and Tyler McPeak, a hulking linebacker, were also dressed for the pep rally. Tyler always tried to imitate Billy's leadership style, but never seemed to be able to pull it off.

Billy held his football helmet upside down. It was filled with slips of paper with the names of the KAOS players and their first victims. "Yo, listen up," he said impatiently, "I have to get to the rally."

"Yeah, listen up," said Tyler.

"When I call your name, take the piece of paper I give you and look at the name written inside," said Billy. "That's your victim. Don't let anybody see it. When you 'kill' your victim, he gives you his piece of paper with the name of the guy he was after. Pretty soon, there are only two people left. If you 'kill' the guy who has your name, you win. That's the way it works."

"That's the way it works," Tyler repeated.

"There are only two other rules," said Billy. "One: You have to kill your victim in a public place. Two: No killing at Murphy."

"Man, that's stupid! Why can't we ice them in school?" said Derek Johnson, a huge senior who was a

22

heavyweight on the wrestling team.

"Yeah," the others chorused.

"You all stupid or something?" Billy demanded. "What if a teacher sees you squirting somebody? He takes your gun away, and game's over."

"Yeah," Dave agreed, "we can't do it at Murphy."

"That settled? Good," said Billy. "Come up when I call you."

Kwame watched as Billy picked a piece of paper from the hat and handed it to Tyler. When it was his turn, Kwame shoved the paper in his pocket without looking at it, and ran to the gym to catch up with his class.

He sprinted down the empty hallways, but slowed to a casual walk when he passed the large window in front of the main office. Kwame waved at the secretary, who smiled and waved back. Once past the window, he started to break into a run again, but his eye was attracted to a colorful brochure that was tacked onto the activities bulletin board.

SUMMER INTERNSHIPS read the bold headline. Among the offerings the brochure advertised were a high school–level program in marine biology, another in computer science, and a German language program in Frankfurt. But the listing that caught Kwame's eye was the one at the bottom. It seemed to have been written specifically for him: a month-long African-American history internship hosted by an Ivy League school.

He ran into the office and approached the secretary. "How do I apply for those summer internships?" he said breathlessly.

"You have to get an application from your guidance counselor," she said.

"Is Mrs. Brewer in?"

"She didn't come in today," the secretary informed him. "But she'll be here tomorrow." She flipped a page on her schedule book and wrote down a time for him to meet with the counselor. She handed him a reminder slip. Kwame thanked her and rushed out the door again.

When Kwame put the note in his pocket, he felt the piece of paper Billy had given him. He hoped his victim wasn't Steve—he would hate to have to eliminate his friend from the game. He opened the slip of paper and gulped at the name of his victim: It was the wrestler, Derek Johnson.

"I hope he's a good sport," Kwame muttered as he entered the gymnasium.

Four

Jennifer Wilson found the Gordon cousins sitting in the bleachers with Cindy. It was Jennifer who had taken her mother's car over a month ago without permission and had had the accident that led to Sarah's coma. After that Jennifer had been grounded for a whole month.

"I heard you had a fight with the boys at 18 Pine yesterday," Jennifer said to them.

Cindy, Tasha, and Sarah all tried to tell her at once.

Jennifer laughed. "Come with me to the bathroom," she said, pointing toward the girls' locker room, "You can tell me on the way."

In the locker room, Debby Barnes, the leader of the Murphy High pep squad, was chatting with Amanda Dennis and Linda Plunkett as they got into their uniforms.

Despite Sarah's efforts to be nice, Debby and her friends had always been rude to the Gordon cousins

25

and their group. Debby hung out only with girls as snobby as she was, and it seemed to irk her that Sarah and Tasha and the rest of the 18 Pine St. gang were so well liked and had so much fun together. Not long ago, Debby's gang had spread the rumor that Cindy wanted to sleep with a certain boy. The trouble her story had caused was a memory she relished.

Linda, a new girl on the pep squad, stopped talking when the four girls walked past. Amanda looked at Sarah and whispered something in Debby's ear that made the pep squad leader giggle.

"What a bunch of fools," Tasha murmured as they headed for the bathroom stalls.

"What did you say?" Debby called out.

"Nothing to you," Tasha shot back.

"Better not," said Debby.

Tasha was about to respond when Sarah gripped her arm and shook her head. "Ignore them," she whispered.

But Debby came out from between the lockers. "Feeling better, Sarah?" she asked.

"Fine," said Sarah neutrally.

"That's good," Debby said, pretending to sound relieved. "Dave was so worried about you when you were in the hospital. I don't think he knew what he was doing. You shouldn't blame him for what happened between us."

Sarah kept walking. Ignore her, she told herself.

"Maybe in your dreams, honey," Tasha piped up. She cocked her head and looked at Debby critically.

26

"Dave wouldn't waste his time with you."

"I'd turn him down, anyway," Debby retorted, "just like I turned down Billy Turner. I go for men, not little boys who date little girls."

"You *don't* want me to get mad," said Tasha, giving Debby an icy stare. "You dis me or my cousin again, I'll hang my foot up your—" Sarah grabbed her cousin's arm and pulled her away before she could finish the sentence.

"Hey, Jennifer, do you want to go to the mall with us this afternoon?" Amanda called out. "Or are you still grounded?"

Debby giggled.

Jennifer's response was a string of curses.

"The mouths on some people," said Debby, shaking her head.

Debby and her friends finished getting dressed. "Don't be late, children," she shouted, pounding on the door of Sarah's bathroom stall. Linda and Amanda laughed loudly as they ran out of the locker room.

"I'm gonna have to hurt Debby Barnes one of these days," said Tasha, drying her hands on a paper towel.

"Just ignore her," said Sarah. "Just think, once Thanksgiving break rolls around, we won't see her for five days!"

"If she lives that long," murmured Jennifer. Tasha nodded.

The band had taken its position on the platform behind the microphone, and the sounds of tuning instruments filled the gymnasium.

Mr. Schlesinger faced the crowd of students in the bleachers and held his hand up. When total silence didn't follow, he cleared his throat into the microphone. "People...people...settle down, now," he said. "As you know, tonight the Murphy High School football team will be hosting the team from Silver Springs."

The students booed at the mention of the rival school and began to stomp on the floorboards. "The winner of that game goes on to the state playoffs," Mr. Schlesinger continued. "But this pep rally is not just for the football team. It is for all the teams that make up the Murphy High School community. At this time I would like to ask the members of the boys' swim team to stand up and take a bow."

The swimmers stood up and waited awkwardly for the applause to die down. Mr. Schlesinger then asked the girls' swim team to take a bow. One by one, he named all the high school teams: baseball, basketball, wrestling.... By the time he got to girls' soccer, the applause was scarce and halfhearted, even from the teachers.

"I can't believe it," Cindy whispered to Sarah. "He actually made the pep rally boring!"

When Mr. Schlesinger called Debby Barnes to the microphone, and backed away himself, the audience applauded enthusiastically.

The rest of the pep squad joined Debby on the floor.

"Hey, you fans! In the stands! If you're with us, clap

28

your hands!" Debby shouted. She clapped out a rhythm for the audience to repeat. The audience clapped back.

In a short time the pep squad had revived the students.

I have to give them credit, Sarah thought grudgingly. The band struck up a funky version of the Murphy High fight song as Debby and the rest of the pep squad cartwheeled, danced, and strutted to the beat. Another fast-paced song followed, and soon the crowd's cheers were at a feverish pitch. By the time the cheerleaders lifted up a huge paper banner showing the high school mascot, Wally the Goat, butting a hapless Silver Springs player into the air, the students were on their feet.

Billy Turner, with the rest of the red-and-gold-clad football team behind him, ran out of the guys' locker room and burst through the paper banner. They set themselves up in an offense formation in the middle of the gymnasium. Suddenly a group of players rushed at a surprised Coach Green and hoisted him onto their shoulders. As they ran a victory lap with the coach aloft, other players gestured to the crowd, beckoning them to scream even louder.

Mr. Schlesinger looked on, slightly bewildered. He watched the mayhem as long as he could, then cleared his throat into the microphone and announced that the pep rally was over. But pandemonium ruled, and it took fifteen minutes to quiet everyone down. By then it was time to go home.

As the crowd milled around the doors of the gym,

Jennifer tapped Tasha's shoulder and pointed to Debby. Debby was talking to Jimmy Walls next to the bandstand. She flirted shamelessly, rubbing one leg behind the other, rustling her pom-poms, and giggling at everything he said.

"Give me a break," whispered Tasha.

Jennifer had a faraway look in her eye. "Watch this," she said suddenly. She ran behind Debby, up to the bandstand, where a chubby black freshman was putting away his sheet music. The tuba he played lay next to his chair.

"Hi!" she said, fixing her gaze on the boy's startled face. She pointed back at Tasha, Cindy, and Sarah. "My friends thought you were the best player in the band."

The chubby boy looked at the girls and grinned. "Well, I . . . I went to camp," he said bashfully.

Jennifer returned his awkward smile with a dazzling one of her own. "Um, do you think I could try it? I mean, just one note? My friends didn't think you would let me."

"Here," he said, helping her lift the tuba. He taught her how to purse her lips as she blew. To the boy's surprise, Jennifer walked toward Debby with the instrument.

Jimmy Walls saw Jennifer approaching, and tried to warn Debby in time, but she was too busy talking. Jennifer got within two feet of the cheerleader and blew a deafening BLAT! that sent Debby into the air with a shriek.

Sarah, Cindy, and Tasha couldn't see Debby's face, but Jimmy must have thought it was the funniest expression he'd ever seen. He burst into loud laughter. Debby whirled around and saw Jennifer handing the tuba back to the bewildered freshman. Her friends were laughing almost as loudly as Jimmy was.

Debby cursed at the girls from 18 Pine St. as she stormed off.

"The mouths on some people!" said Jennifer, with a tsk-tsk sound.

PINE

Five

True to his word, Mr. Harris had begun repainting the back wall of 18 Pine St. When the gang walked into the pizza parlor, shaking a light dusting of snow from their coats, they were surprised to see a cord taped along the back booths to prevent anyone from sitting in them. The back wall had been scrubbed, and patches of plaster were visible where Mr. Harris had covered over the names and words that had been gouged into the wall over the years.

Kwame looked impressed as he surveyed the work Mr. Harris had done. "Harris don't play," he murmured to Sarah and Tasha.

The three sat down with Cindy and April. Steve and Dave joined them a few minutes later.

When Billy arrived he was grinning broadly. "Well, Rashad is out of the game," he said.

"Where did you get him?" the boys asked.

"I saw him walking home from school with his buddies, and I drove past really slow. I didn't even get out of the car. Boy never knew what hit him!" He raised his hand over the middle of the table, and Dave, Steve, and Kwame high-fived him.

"That's disgusting!" Tasha cried.

"Like a drive-by shooting!" said Sarah.

"You guys are sick," said Cindy.

April Winter, who was Steve's girlfriend, gave a quick shudder that made her blond hair fall in front of her eyes. Without a word, she moved her chair away from Steve's side and joined the rest of the girls on the opposite end of the table.

"Rashad ain't dead!" said Billy. "He's just out of the game."

"Yeah, he's just off the chessboard," said Kwame.

"Chess is totally different, and you know it," said Tasha vehemently. "Chess is about strategy and using your brains. Any fool can sneak up on someone and shoot him with a water gun." She looked directly at Billy. "You're worse than those kids in L.A. we saw in that movie. At least they had to fight to survive."

"Yeah," April piped up, "what's your excuse?"

"It's a water gun!" Billy said, almost yelling. "We're playing a game. You know: pretend?" he said sarcastically. The other boys laughed.

"Even if it is pretend, it's still violent," said Sarah. Dave rolled his eyes, which made Sarah bristle even more.

Kwame stirred the ice in his cup with his straw. "Playing violent and being violent are two different things," he said. "Most games are violent in one way or another. I've seen you play basketball, Tasha, and you can get pretty rough."

Tasha shook her head. "Totally different, Kwame," she replied. "In basketball the object isn't to, quote, kill somebody. It's to score points."

"I think this is one of those male things," said Dave. "No matter what we say, you females are not going to see our side." His friends nodded in agreement. "And we're not going to see yours. So let's just change the subject."

"No, let's just change tables," said Sarah, getting up. Cindy, Tasha, and April looked at her in surprise, but they followed her lead. The boys laughed nervously as each girl took her cup, coat, and backpack to a table near the picture window.

"I don't believe this," said Dave, looking over at them.

José Melendez walked into the pizzeria and looked back and forth between the two tables. He flipped his straight black hair away from his eyes and looked at the girls for an explanation. When José assured them he was not in the game, they invited him to sit down.

Dave frowned. Not long ago, José Melendez and Sarah had dated for a while. It hadn't worked out, and they'd decided to remain good friends. Still it gnawed at Dave that José was sitting with his girlfriend.

"They made their point," Steve grumbled as he

35

looked at the table where April sat. "Why don't they come back?"

"They're trying to punish us," said Billy scornfully. "Let's not give in to 'em."

"No way!" the boys agreed. They talked about KAOS, the pep rally, and the upcoming football game. Soon, however, the conversation faded into an uncomfortable silence.

Billy stood up. "I have to go," he said. "Big game tonight."

"Try not to play too violently," said Steve, mimicking a girl's voice. The boys laughed.

As Billy gathered his things to go, Kwame opened his backpack and took out his history homework. "Great!" he mumbled. His bright green water pistol had leaked onto the cover of the textbook. He pulled out the gun and was startled by the sight of Dave, Steve, and Billy rearing back from the table. Kwame laughed at them. "It's okay, guys, I'm just getting my book out."

"Hey, no water guns in here!" Mr. Harris called out from the counter.

Embarrassed, Kwame put the gun back in his book bag.

"New rule," said Billy. "You can't shoot at 18 Pine."

"That's a relief," said Steve with a sigh. They said good-bye to Billy and watched him walk past the group of girls without looking at them. Only José waved as he left.

"You two going to the game tonight?" Steve asked,

36

turning back to the table. Kwame and Dave nodded.

"I was supposed to drive Sarah, Cindy, and Tasha to school tonight," said Dave. "After all this, I may be going alone."

"Me too," said Steve, looking at April.

"Serves you two right," said Kwame, looking down at his book. "You should have stayed single like me!"

When Tasha and Sarah returned home, Miss Essie informed them that Mr. and Mrs. Gordon had still not decided where to go on their vacation. Mr. Gordon had tried to push his ski trip by leaving brochures lying on top of the coffee table. But Mrs. Gordon had come home that afternoon carrying a new one-piece bathing suit made from a shiny red fabric. "We'll get a cabin with a hot tub," Mr. Gordon promised. "You can wear it there."

Sarah and Tasha went to Miss Essie's room after dinner to help her pack for New York. "Whew, what's in here?" said Tasha, hefting one of the two suitcases.

"Makeup and hair things, mostly," said Miss Essie, without turning away from the dresser.

"You shouldn't carry this heavy bag all by yourself," Tasha protested. "It weighs a ton. You're going to hurt yourself."

"No, I'm not," said her grandmother. "You can put it in the car for me, and your uncle will take it to the baggage counter at the airport. Once I'm in New York, the redcap will take it to the cab, the cabby will put it in the car, and the bellboy will put it in the hotel room."

37

"You have it all figured out," said Sarah with a laugh.

"I hope you tip them well," said Tasha, lifting the suitcase again.

Sarah called Jennifer that evening to tell her what had happened at 18 Pine St., how she and the other girls had moved to another table.

"It's a sick game. Those boys had it coming," said Jennifer.

"I know," said Sarah with a sigh. "But maybe I over-reacted."

"You didn't," said Jennifer, "and April, Tasha, and Cindy will back me up."

"It's just that I miss Dave. I was supposed to go to the game with him." She paused. "Maybe Dave and I can agree to disagree about this. My parents can't agree on where to go for their vacation, but they're still talking to each other."

"Yeah, but they're married," said Jennifer with a laugh, "they have to get along. You still going to the game tonight?"

"I don't know," said Sarah. "How about you?"

"No," Jennifer grumbled. "I've got a math test coming up. I need to study."

After they hung up, Sarah dialed Dave's number.

Tasha saw her in the hallway. "You calling him?"

Sarah nodded as the phone rang at Dave's house. "I can't help it," she said.

"Well, I'm not having anything to do with Billy until he's out of that stupid game," Tasha said firmly.

The phone rang a second time at Dave's house.

"You got to stick up for what you believe, cuz," added Tasha, "especially if you know you're right."

"Okay, you made your point!" said Sarah, putting the phone down.

"I'm proud of you." Tasha beamed. "I know what it took to do that." She put her arm around her cousin. "It's only until he's out of the game," she said sympathetically.

PINE

Six

Things were going poorly for the Murphy High football team. Under the glare of the floodlights, the field looked like a huge muddy doormat. The Silver Springs team had a comfortable 27–14 lead at halftime, and despite the pep squad's efforts, the crowd had lost its enthusiasm.

Halfway up the bleachers, Cindy, April, and the Gordons huddled under a blanket. Sarah saw Kwame, Steve, and Dave sitting with a large group of boys near the Murphy High end zone, not far from the snack hut. They looked as if they were having a good time. Sarah missed Dave. She decided to buy a cup of hot chocolate, in the hope that he would call after her. Tasha couldn't get mad if Sarah talked to him just to be polite!

She was about to stand up when she saw Dave suddenly leave his friends. He dashed up the half-empty bleachers, pulled out a plastic gun, and squirted a boy named Mike Sherry in the back of the neck. Mike, who

41

had been sitting with his two younger brothers, jumped up, angrily wiping his neck. When he saw Dave he started to curse before he remembered it was part of the game. He grudgingly pulled out a slip of paper from his pocket and handed it to Dave. When Dave returned from his mission, Kwame, Steve, and the other boys slapped him on the back. Sarah watched as Mike explained to his brothers that he'd just been assassinated.

"Did you see that?" Sarah cried to her friends. They had not. She described the kill to them. "They're acting like a group of third-graders playing superheroes," she said angrily.

"I told you what I'm doing, cuz: no dating, no nothing until Billy's out of the game," said Tasha.

"That's a good idea," said April, looking at Steve.

"Yes!" said Sarah.

Sarah didn't feel the cold as much in the second half. The bulky layers of clothing and her father's polar ski gloves were warm, but the excitement of the game helped too. She kept jumping up to cheer a revived Murphy High team. The crack of helmets and plastic pads echoed across the field in the last grueling minutes. The score at the final buzzer was 35–35, and it didn't change in the overtime.

Suddenly Tasha ran down to the players' bench, where Billy stood with his helmet under his arm. His face was drenched in sweat, and he drank cup after cup of Gatorade.

"Way to go, Turner!" said Tasha.

Billy grinned back at her.

Immediately Sarah ran down after Tasha. "I thought you weren't going to talk to him," she said.

Tasha shrugged. "It's a sports thing. He brought our team back from defeat; I had to give him credit for that."

"How cute!" said a voice behind them.

Tasha and Sarah turned. Debby Barnes and her friends stood on the sidelines. They all wore white leggings, red wool skirts that came down to their knees, and gold sweaters with a big red "M" on the front. Despite the cold Debby looked comfortable and stylish. She smirked at the sight of Sarah in her bulky clothes. She seemed especially amused by Mr. Gordon's oversized gloves.

Sarah knew there was nothing to feel embarrassed about, but she felt her face getting warm anyway. Debby had a knack for making people feel uncomfortable.

"Do you mind?" Tasha said. "I was talking to my cousin."

"Go ahead, I'm just standing here," said Debby nonchalantly.

When Jimmy Walls walked by, Debby gave him a big hug. He clumsily hugged her back in his football uniform. Out of the corner of her eye, Sarah could see Steve Adams sneaking up on Jimmy. Abruptly Jimmy wrestled free of Debby and took off. Debby lost her footing and fell down.

It was a comical scene: a big football player running away from a skinny white guy with a bright red squirt gun—not to mention Debby's going splat in the mud.

"I know who you are," Jimmy yelled back at Steve. "You'll never get me now, homeboy!"

Steve saw he couldn't catch him and he gave up running. He walked dejectedly back to Kwame and Dave. Billy joined them for a second in the stands.

"What was that all about?" said Linda Plunkett, helping Debby up.

"Welcome to KAOS, girls," said Sarah. She explained the game to them. "Jimmy is in it, and so is Marc Halle," she said, referring to a boy Linda liked.

"We're not having anything to do with them until they quit," said Tasha. "Well, almost nothing."

"I'm down for that," said Debby. She craned her neck to see the back of her skirt. Her fall had blotted a broad stain of mud onto the fabric and her white leggings were flecked with dirt and wet grass. "Bunch of idiots," she muttered, wiping the back of her skirt. Jimmy came back to apologize, but Debby told him to leave her alone.

Sarah took her cousin's arm and started toward the concession stand, where April and Cindy were waiting for them.

"We saw everything," they said.

"Debby is a pain in the rear," Tasha told them. "She had that fall coming."

They all nodded, but Sarah felt a twinge of sympathy for Debby. She didn't like her, but underneath all

44

Debby's petty words and actions, Sarah suspected there was one unhappy girl.

Tasha saw Sarah's expression and shook her head. "Sarah, don't be feeling sorry for her—you're such a goody-goody sometimes."

"No I'm not," Sarah murmured. But Sarah knew her cousin was right. It wasn't the first time she'd been called a goody-goody and it probably wouldn't be the last.

Kwame had enjoyed the hard-fought football game. But even as he sat in the bleachers cheering, with his friends, his mind had been on the African-American history internship.

The following morning, he went to his guidance counselor's office at the appointed hour and waited for Mrs. Brewer.

Mrs. Brewer motioned Kwame into her office. The first thing Kwame noticed about her was that her hair, once frizzy brown and tied back in a bun, had been cut short and dyed black. It looked like a helmet. He looked away before she could catch him staring at it.

"What can I do for you today, Mr. Brown?" she said pleasantly. She always addressed her students as Mister and Ms.

"I saw that flyer in the hallway for the summer internships, and I came to pick up an application," he said, barely suppressing his enthusiasm.

Mrs. Brewer reached into her desk and pulled out a file. "Wonderful, Mr. Brown. Which program are you interested in: marine biology, German, or computer science?"

"African-American history," he said without hesitation.

"That's what I was afraid of," she said, almost to herself. She closed the folder and looked at Kwame. The smile on her face had dimmed, and her eyes displayed a vague concern. "Mr. Brown," she began softly, "the reason they're offering that program is to attract blacks to their school. I called the college, and they told me the African-American history internship is an affirmative action project."

Kwame shrugged. "So?"

Mrs. Brewer picked up her coffee cup and sipped thoughtfully. "As you know, Mr. Brown, the government set up the affirmative action program to make sure that companies, colleges, and government offices don't discriminate against minorities." She looked at Kwame. "Can you tell me what percent of Americans are black?"

"Twelve percent," said Kwame, without hesitation.

"That's right," she said. "And affirmative action's goal is to have companies and colleges reflect that percentage. The leaders of this program want to be sure blacks and other minorities are fairly represented in all employment, educational, and social programs."

"So the African-American history internship is designed to bring blacks to that college. What's wrong with that?" Kwame asked.

"I'm thinking of your self-respect, Mr. Brown," said

46

Mrs. Brewer firmly. "Can you respect yourself if you know that the only reason you would be allowed in the program is because you're a minority?"

"No," said Kwame. "But that wouldn't be the only reason they'd let me in. I have good grades and I really want to learn more about African-American history! I'm crazy about the Civil War. You should see my room. I have this collection of battle maps from—"

"That's wonderful, Mr. Brown," the counselor interrupted him. "But I don't think you're getting my point. You are one of the smartest students in your grade, especially in social studies. But if you get accepted to this program, it isn't because you're good at history; it's only because you're black and they need blacks."

She held up an application for the marine biology internship, which had a picture of a coral reef in the top corner. "Some colleges are afraid that black students won't apply for an internship like this, so they offer one in African-American history. This will attract enough students so that the college can meet its obligations to maintain fair minority representation."

Kwame looked at the African-American brochure. He immediately recognized Martin Luther King, Jr., Booker T. Washington, and Frederick Douglass, but there were two figures he didn't know—two imposing women who seemed to be staring directly at him. The unknowns piqued his curiosity. He wasn't interested in the issue of affirmative action; he just wanted that history internship. He felt like grabbing the application and running out the door.

Mrs. Brewer put the application back in the folder. "I'm thinking about your self-image, Kwame," she said, using his first name for the first time. "I don't want one of Murphy High's best students to be judged by whites as being inferior. They'll think the only reason you're in the summer program at that elite Ivy League school is because they had to take you."

"What do I care what they think?" Kwame almost shouted. "Let them think what they want; I'll know better. Isn't that the only thing that counts?"

"No," said Mrs. Brewer firmly. "You see, it's not just you they'd be judging, it's all blacks. As long as whites see us as getting into these colleges through the 'back door' of affirmative action, we'll all be considered charity cases. You're too smart for that. I don't want them to think of you that way."

"So what am I supposed to do—not go?" said Kwame. "I really wanted to do this!"

"Have you thought about applying for an internship at a black university?" said Mrs. Brewer.

Kwame shook his head. He felt vaguely guilty for not considering the option, especially since his plan had always been to apply to Howard University in his senior year. "I didn't see any brochures about internships at black schools up on the activities bulletin board," he said defensively.

"We'll have to see if they offer the same type of program," Mrs. Brewer said.

"What if they don't?" Kwame challenged.

48

"Let me look into it," said Mrs. Brewer. "In the meantime," she said, pulling out the folder again, "you could look over these. According to my files, you're aceing math and science again this year." She handed him two applications: one for computer science, another for marine biology. "The representative of the internship program will be here next week," she said. "So get the applications back to me as soon as possible."

Kwame took the applications and put them in his book bag without looking at them.

Mrs. Brewer got up and walked him to the door. "Keep up the good work, Mr. Brown," she said as he left.

Kwame walked slowly through the empty hallways, his mind buzzing with a hundred different thoughts. He knew he was nobody's charity case, and he didn't understand how any white person could hurt his self-esteem. "I get better grades than they do!" he said. His voice echoed off the rows of lockers.

He pushed open the door to the guys' rest room, unzipping his book bag as he headed to the trash can near the sinks. The applications were made of a heavy, cream-colored paper—they made a dull, ripping sound as Kwame tore them up.

PINE

Seven

The lunch trays were still hot from the dishwasher when Sarah picked one from the stack in the cafeteria. She looked at the menu: cream of mushroom soup, spaghetti with meat sauce, creamed corn, and applesauce. It was what some Murphy High students called a Bad Food Day. At least the soup crackers will be crunchy, she thought.

Sarah saw only boys at their usual table but spied Cindy waving to her from a table at the opposite end of the cafeteria. Jennifer, April, and Tasha were already there.

"Spread out," said April, putting her feet on the empty chair next to her. "We've got all the room in the world today."

"Yeah. It's girls' night out," said Jennifer as Sarah sat down.

"You don't miss Robert?" said Sarah, referring to Jennifer's most recent romantic interest. Jennifer had

51

two classes with him this semester, and the two of them had begun to hang out. Robert was a funny guy with a reputation for being a class clown. Recently Jennifer had discovered that Robert's parents were founding members of the exclusive Madison Tennis and Swim Club.

"Robert who?" said Jennifer. "Do you miss Dave?"

"Dave who?" said Sarah. "Hey, Tasha, do you miss Billy?"

"Billy who?" said Tasha with a laugh.

At that moment Debby Barnes, Linda Plunkett, and Amanda Dennis approached their table. They put their lunch trays on the table and sat down.

"Hi, girls," said Debby casually, as if they always ate together. "What's up?"

"What's up with you?" said Cindy.

"Not much. Had a killer test in math this morning," said Debby blandly as she poked her fork into the spaghetti.

Sarah and Tasha traded curious looks. What do they want? Sarah wondered. She knew Debby was up to something because the pep squad leader had gone out of her way to say hello in the halls that morning. Now, instead of flirting at the table where the football players sat, they had come to sit where they knew they were not welcome.

"Anything we can do for you?" said Tasha.

"Yeah," Cindy piped up. "We were kind of having a private talk."

"You all go on," said Debby. "We just want to talk to

52

Sarah." Debby turned to face her. "You know that KAOS thing Dave is playing?"

Sarah nodded. The whole school knew by now, and rumors about who had been eliminated and who was still in the game were circulating in the hallways. The football game had been a major "killing" ground. Besides Mike Sherry, two other students had been "shot" there. Sarah had hoped that Dave would be one of the early casualties, but he had a flair for the game, and was already on his third victim.

"I have a KAOS game that makes theirs look like kid stuff," Debby went on proudly. "It's called KAOS too."

"Great!" Tasha muttered sarcastically. "Like we don't have enough killing games."

"Not killing, kissing," corrected Linda Plunkett.

"Kissing KAOS," added Amanda Dennis.

April, Tasha, Jennifer, and Sarah listened as Debby explained the rules of the new game. "Each girl names a boyfriend," she said. "The way you eliminate a player from the game is by kissing her boyfriend. The winner is the girl whose boyfriend holds out the longest."

"But you have to kiss them in public," said Amanda.

"And you can't tell your boyfriends about the game," added Linda.

"What a stupid game," said Tasha, giggling.

"I don't blame you for not liking it." Debby looked at her coolly. "It'd be too easy to kiss Billy."

"Jimmy Walls would do it before Billy," challenged

Tasha.

Debby ignored this, and turned her attention to Sarah. "What do you think?"

"No, thanks, Debby. I don't think Dave would like it."

Amanda rolled her eyes. "Did Dave care what you thought about the killing game?"

The words hit Sarah with surprising force. She remembered how disgusted she had been the night before, watching Dave sneak up on Mike Sherry in the stands. The more she thought about it, the more indignant she felt. It would serve the boys right, she thought. And if Dave gets upset, well, then that's even better. He'll know firsthand how I feel about his dumb game.

"Okay, I'm in," Sarah said impulsively. Debby and Tasha's eyebrows shot up. They both looked surprised that "goody-goody" Sarah Gordon would do something like this.

"I'm in, too," said Jennifer.

Tasha, after a few moments of hesitation, agreed to play as well.

April said nothing at first. Debby was acting friendly now, but April could still remember the day the leader of the pep squad had accused her of trying to act black because she spent so much time hanging out with Sarah and her friends. Debby Barnes usually meant trouble, and April didn't want to get involved. "Not me," she said finally.

"Name your boyfriends," Debby said, barely

acknowledging April's response. "Jimmy Walls." She pointed to herself.

"Dave Hunter," said Sarah.

"Billy Turner," said Tasha.

"Marc Halle," said Linda.

"Robert Thornton," said Jennifer.

"Tyler McPeak," said Amanda.

"This is going to be fun," said Debby. "But don't forget the two rules: Don't tell the boys, and all kisses have to be in public."

They spent the rest of the lunch period talking and bragging about how they were going to get each other's boyfriends. Sarah wasn't worried about Dave. It was just one kiss—how could that make him fall for any of the girls at her table? Yet she began to wonder how Dave would react if he saw her kiss another guy in public.

Sarah was distracted from these thoughts by the laughter of the group. It surprised her to see how the whole table was getting along. Maybe the guys playing KAOS had brought the girls together for once.

In her customary theatrical style, Miss Essie had sent a telegram from New York to her family to announce the results of her audition. It was posted on the refrigerator door with a magnet when Tasha and Sarah got home. "GOT IT. ESSIE" was all it said. The cousins whooped and gave each other high-fives.

"I knew she'd get that commercial," said Tasha proudly.

"Go ahead, Miss Essie," said Sarah, pouring herself a glass of Kool-Aid. "Allison, did you see this?" she said to her sister, who had just come into the room.

"Who do you think put it up?" Allison replied. She took her older sister's glass of Kool-Aid from the counter. "Thanks," she said.

Sarah gave Allison a stern look and poured herself another glass. "Have you learned your part for the Thanksgiving play yet?" she asked.

Allison rolled her eyes. "Days ago!" she said. She launched into a speech about the importance of corn to the Native Americans and to the first white settlers.

When she finished, Sarah and Tasha applauded.

"You should think about becoming an actress, like Miss Essie," said Tasha.

Eight

Kwame was surprised to see his target at the Westcove Mall on Saturday. Kwame was meeting Steve there to play video games, after they'd sworn to each other on the phone that neither one was the other's intended KAOS victim.

Derek Johnson was walking with an older woman who, Kwame guessed, must be his mother. Derek wore his red-and-gold wrestling jacket and a pair of black jeans that were tight around his stocky legs. Kwame nervously touched the water gun in his pocket. He suddenly wished he hadn't brought it along, although it was part of the game's allure to be "armed and ready" to meet the victim.

He followed Derek and his mother through the mall for fifteen minutes, ducking into stores whenever they looked in his direction. From behind a fountain, Kwame watched with a mixture of fear and awe as Derek ate four hamburgers at the food court. With

Derek sitting down and distracted by the food, it would have been the ideal time to shoot. As he approached their table, Derek lifted his cup of iced tea to his mouth.

"Maybe later," Kwame told himself. He put the gun back in his pocket and ducked into the video arcade.

Noise from electronic tanks, race cars, and explosions surrounded Kwame as he wandered inside the dark game hall. He found Steve in front of the only game he ever played: Open Season.

Kwame leaned against the broken machine next to it and watched his friend. He had accumulated two extra Duck Hunters. The firing button fluttered up and down under Steve's fingers as he electronically shot down the flying bomb-laden ducks that threatened the hunter on the video screen. When the last bomber duck in the flight pattern came down with a mechanical squawk, music sounded, and a new army of ducks appeared on the horizon.

"If I get these, I'll have another hunter," said Steve. "Then you can take over for a round."

"Thanks, man," said Kwame.

For a split second, Kwame thought a bug had flown into his ear. He heard a guffaw, and became aware of water trickling down his neck. Rubbing his wet ear, he looked to his right and saw Tyler McPeak, the linebacker from the football team, with an Uzi-shaped water pistol in his hand.

"Kwame, man, you should have seen your face," said Tyler.

Kwame stole a glance at Steve, who was staring at his video game and acting as if he hadn't seen or heard anything.

"Who's next, Kwame, my man?" Tyler asked.

Kwame dug out the slip of paper with Derek Johnson's name and handed it to Tyler.

"Hey, I saw you following him," said Tyler, when he saw the name on the paper. "How come you didn't ice him?"

"Couldn't get a clear shot," Kwame mumbled.

"I will," Tyler assured him. Before he left, he pulled out his plastic Uzi and squirted Steve in the back, soaking his T-shirt. "Oops. Sorry, dude," he said with a laugh.

Steve didn't turn around, but he blushed a violent red and tapped the buttons on the machine even harder. "I'm not the guy he was after, so I'm still in the game," he told Kwame.

"I know," said Kwame. "Tyler's just being a jerk." Kwame wiped the last drop of water out of his ear and smiled in spite of himself. Kwame was secretly relieved that he was out of the game. Tracking and shooting victims like Derek Johnson and Tyler McPeak wasn't as much fun as it had seemed at the beginning of the game.

"Hey, look!" someone shouted.

Kwame heard frightened shouts and crashing noises. They weren't coming from any game.

"Be right back," he called to Steve as he ran to the entrance that faced the food court. A crowd was gathering around two massive teenagers who were rolling on the ground. It didn't take long to figure out what had happened.

When Tyler McPeak had left the video arcade, he wasted no time going after his next victim. He must have spied Derek sitting with his mother at the same plastic table near the fountain, and fired. Now the two of them were locked together on the floor. Tyler was two inches taller, and he outweighed Derek by twenty pounds, but Derek somehow managed to force himself on top of the other guy. He dug his knee into Tyler's back. Tyler yelled and bucked, knocking Derek off him. Both stood up quickly, breathing heavily. Tyler charged at Derek, aiming low as he had learned to do in football practice.

"Derek," shouted Mrs. Johnson. "Stop this!"

But Derek was just getting started. "Come on!" he snarled. He crouched and waited for the impact, his hands jerking like pincers on a crab.

When the two collided, Derek was thrown to the floor. He managed to wriggle out of Tyler's grip. The two boys quickly got up and circled each other menacingly.

Kwame felt himself being pushed aside as two mall security guards broke through the crowd. They were middle-aged men in white shirts, with walkie-talkies clipped to their belts.

With lightning speed, Derek grabbed Tyler's arm and pinned it behind his back. Tyler struggled to free himself, but Derek held firm. Grunting, Derek lifted Tyler onto his shoulder and staggered toward the fountain. When Tyler saw what Derek had in mind, he flailed his legs furiously, and Derek lost his balance. The crowd gasped as both boys tumbled into the shallow water.

Four more mall security guards rushed forward. With three guards pulling on each drenched boy, they managed to separate the fighters. The last Kwame saw of them, they were being led to a security office near the rest rooms.

Kwame returned to the video arcade, more relieved than ever to be out of the game. He found Steve exactly where he had left him: punching the buttons on Open Season. José Melendez was nearby, watching.

"What did we miss?" said Steve, stepping aside to let Kwame take over the controls.

"Tyler and Derek had a fight," said Kwame.

"Awesome!" said José. "Why? What happened? Who won?"

"The security guards broke it up," said Kwame. "But Derek had the upper hand. He tried to throw Tyler in the fountain."

"Wow!" said Steve. He pulled his damp T-shirt away from his back. "What else happened?"

"I'll tell you in a minute," said Kwame quickly. His attention was fixed on a duck that was coming toward his hunter with an egg bomb. It felt good to be shooting at electronic enemies rather than hulking football players who took KAOS very seriously.

18
PINE

Nine

On Monday morning Sarah saw Dave at his locker. She found herself automatically walking toward him before she remembered the promise she'd made with the other girls. She stopped, turned, and pretended to look for something in her book bag. Dave tapped her on the shoulder.

"What's up?" he said brightly.

Before Sarah could answer him, Tasha appeared at her elbow. Be strong, her cousin's eyes seemed to be saying. Sarah gave Dave a neutral look. "Not much. What's up with you?"

"I've got to hand in that English paper—" He broke off when he saw the hostile look on Tasha's face. "I'll catch up with you later," he told Sarah. He walked off without a smile.

"I'm proud of you," said Tasha with a grin.

"Did you see how upset he looked?" Sarah wailed.

"He'll get over it," Tasha assured her. "Do you realize it could have been Dave in the mall?"

Sarah nodded. She had heard about the big fight from Kwame the day before.

"I told you this whole thing would get out of hand," said Tasha as she walked her cousin to her art class.

When they turned the corner, they saw Dave again. He was drinking from a water fountain, and Debby Barnes was waiting for him to finish. When Dave saw the Gordons again, he gave them a cold look and turned to Debby. Extending one arm against the wall above her head, Dave leaned toward her. Sarah whirled around and stomped into art class.

As Sarah molded her lump of clay into a frog, she brooded about Debby and Dave.

"That's so realistic," Jennifer commented as she appraised Sarah's frog.

"Thanks," said Sarah. She lowered her voice to a whisper. "Have you gotten anybody yet?"

"No," Jennifer whispered back. "But I've got my eye on Tyler McPeak," she said.

"Go for it!" said Sarah. She picked up the frog, placed it on a sheet of paper towel, and gingerly lifted it onto the shelf to dry.

"How about you?" said Jennifer, following her. "Have you got anybody in mind?"

"Jimmy Walls," said Sarah without hesitation.

Sarah saw Jimmy in the lunchroom later that day, but she couldn't summon up the nerve to kiss him.

Tasha knows how to flirt, she thought with a touch of envy. When Sarah had asked her cousin who she was after, Tasha had said Marc Halle.

"Linda Plunkett keeps bragging about what a good kisser he is," said Tasha in a low voice. "I'm going to find out."

"I hope Debby doesn't find out what a good kisser Dave is," Sarah whispered back.

Her eye fell on Kwame, who was sitting directly across from her. He was the only boy at the table, but no one questioned his presence since he was out of the KAOS game. He was sitting with a book perched on his lap, and wore an angry expression.

Sarah whispered to Cindy, "What's he so mad about? I thought it was only a game."

"Beats me," said Cindy. "Hey, Kwame, what's wrong?"

Kwame barely looked up from his book. He waved his hand to indicate he was fine. But when Tasha got up and took a seat next to him, Sarah moved to the empty seat on the other side.

"Do you mind?" he said to the cousins.

"Tell us what's wrong, Kwame," urged April.

"Yeah, who is she?" Cindy chimed in. "We'll scratch her eyes out!"

Kwame forced a weak smile at that. He closed his book and told them about the African-American history internship. "But Mrs. Brewer said it's an affirmative action program, and she doesn't think I should apply for it."

"What's it to her?" Jennifer demanded.

"She thinks it'll hurt my self-esteem because I would only be accepted for being black."

"At least this place is trying to attract blacks," said Sarah. "How many blacks got into a school like that before affirmative action?"

"Mrs. Brewer says I should think about a summer internship at a black school," said Kwame.

"I can't believe she won't even let you apply," said Jennifer. "Someone ought to straighten her out."

Tasha shook her head in disgust. "Affirmative action is supposed to help blacks avoid discrimination. I think Mrs. Brewer is one of those gung-ho people who believe that unless blacks achieve success on their own, without any government help, they'll never be respected. But you can't just turn down an opportunity like this because it's sponsored by affirmative action. If it's right for you, go for it."

"It's too late anyway," said Kwame, his voice cracking. "I haven't filled out an application and the representative from the program is coming to Murphy to talk to the applicants on Thursday."

"Then we don't have much time," said Sarah, standing up. She grabbed Kwame's arm and pulled him out of the chair. The five girls escorted him to the main office.

The secretary was surprised to see them. When they demanded to talk to Mrs. Brewer, the secretary shook her head. "She sees students only by appointment."

"This is very important," Cindy insisted.

While the secretary was busy talking to Cindy and the others, Kwame slipped away and headed down the short hallway that led to the guidance offices. The girls had gotten him fired up. Kwame knocked, and Mrs. Brewer opened the door. Soft music from a radio drifted out of the room.

"Mrs. Brewer, I'm here to get an application for the history internship," said Kwame.

Mrs. Brewer looked surprised. "Mr. Brown, I thought we already discussed this," she said.

"I changed my mind," said Kwame. "I'd like an application anyway."

Mrs. Brewer looked at the girls who now stood behind him. "I think you're making a big mistake," she said firmly. She disappeared into her office. Kwame looked into the room and noticed they had interrupted her lunch. A cup filled with soup steamed on her desk. Mrs. Brewer turned off the radio on top of the file drawer as she looked for the application. She came back with the form and handed it to Kwame. "I wish you had told me about your change of heart sooner," she said. "You don't have much time to write the essay."

"That's okay," said Kwame. He took the paper and looked at the corner. Martin Luther King, Jr., Frederick Douglass, Booker T. Washington, and the two unknown women looked back at him.

Mrs. Brewer closed the door to her office without another word.

After the secretary had sternly reproached the group

for walking past her, Kwame and his friends stopped in the hallway outside the main office. He gave them an awkward smile.

"I really appreciate this," he told them.

"What are friends for?" said Sarah, giving him a quick hug.

Kwame hugged Cindy, too—and Jennifer, April, and finally Tasha, who surprised him by giving him a warm kiss.

That afternoon Sarah's health teacher announced to her students that they would be going next door to watch a film with the other health class. Sarah waved to her friends in the other room as she and the rest of her classmates filed in and took seats along the back wall behind the film projector. The classroom was a little larger than Sarah's, but otherwise it was just like her own. A poster of the food pyramid had been taped to the back wall next to a chart about human sexuality.

Jimmy Walls and Amanda Dennis were both in the other class, Sarah noticed. This is my chance to get Jimmy, she thought as her heart began to beat faster. Jimmy had his desk in the back of the room, and Sarah took a seat next to him.

When Jimmy saw Sarah he flashed her a big smile. "What's up?" he said.

"Hi, Jimmy," she replied. Out of the corner of her eye, she could see Amanda looking at them.

When Mrs. Topolewski walked to the front of the class and announced the name of the movie, *The*

Human Body: Nature's Wonder Machine, she set off a chorus of groans from the students. The other teacher turned off the lights in the back of the room and shushed the class.

The movie opened with a picture of a grinning cartoon automobile. "Your body is like a car in many ways," the narrator announced cheerfully. The class hooted and started yelling out comments, and the teachers warned them to be quiet or they would stop the film.

Now's as good a time as any, Sarah thought. Jimmy's head was thrown back and his arms were folded in front of him. He looked bored. Sarah inched her seat closer to his. She wondered if a quick peck on the cheek in the dark counted as a "public" kiss, and decided it did. I'm in public, she reasoned. I can't help it if they're all looking the other way.

She glanced at the teacher who was monitoring the back of the classroom. He had taken a seat next to the door and was trying to read a book by the light coming in from the hallway.

Jimmy sensed the movement and turned toward Sarah. He grinned at her and leaned over conveniently close to her face. His eyes were closed and his mouth seemed to be inviting hers. Whoa, thought Sarah. This guy's ready for more than a quick peck on the cheek. Just go for it, she told herself as she closed her eyes, pursed her lips, and leaned over.

As she waited for Jimmy's lips to meet hers, Sarah didn't see Amanda walk up to Mrs. Topolewski to tell

69

on her.

"Let's try to pay attention to the movie," said Mrs. Topolewski loudly.

Sarah opened her eyes and sat bolt upright. Jimmy's face was no longer close to hers. He was sitting upright, smirking, and pointing a finger at her. Around them students were giggling. And Amanda Dennis was making her way back to her seat with a smug expression on her face.

Sarah stared at the screen. She tried to ignore the few students who were giggling at her. But her face was hot with shame and fury. Jimmy set me up! How long was I leaning there with my eyes closed and my lips out? she wondered. She was grateful that the lights had been off and that most of the students hadn't seen what had happened. But she knew Amanda would fill everyone in.

The class quieted down again, but now and then, Jimmy made a loud kissing noise that cracked up the class, and made Sarah want to die of embarrassment.

Maybe playing kissing KAOS hadn't been such a good idea after all.

Ten

Sarah went home immediately after school was over. She threw herself into her homework, trying to forget about Jimmy, Debby, and the stupid kissing game. When the phone rang, both she and Tasha ran into the hallway to pick it up. Tasha got there first, and Sarah saw a chilly expression form on her cousin's face.

"Is the game over?" Tasha demanded. "Oh. Well, she can't come to the phone right now, but I'll tell her you called." She hung up before Sarah could grab the phone from her hand.

"That was Dave, wasn't it?" cried Sarah.

"What if it was?" said Tasha casually.

"I'm sick of arguing with him," Sarah stated. "I miss him. Besides, this whole kissing game is stupid—"

Before Sarah could finish telling Tasha about health class, the phone rang again. This time Sarah picked it up.

It was Cindy. "Hey, Sarah, you'd better watch your

back," she warned.

Sarah tried to hide her disappointment. "Hi, Cindy," she said. "Why should I watch my back?"

"I overheard Amanda talking about you this afternoon. She was telling Debby what happened in health today."

"Great. Now the whole school knows!" Sarah said irritably. "Jimmy set me up."

"No, Debby set you up," Cindy went on. "Debby told Jimmy one of us was going to try to kiss him one of these days, and to be on the lookout."

"Are you sure about that?" said Sarah.

"Debby and Amanda are in Francie's study period," said Cindy. "They pretend Francie doesn't exist because she's so overweight and shy. Anyway, Francie heard Amanda say, 'She tried to do it in health class,' and Debby said something like, 'Shoot. I wish she'd tried it in the cafeteria so everybody could have seen it.'"

Sarah felt herself growing more angry by the minute. She should have known not to trust Debby Barnes. "Can I call you back later?" she said, needing time to think things through.

"Sure," Cindy replied.

Sarah hurried to the kitchen. She stopped just outside the swinging door when she heard her parents talking heatedly inside.

"You should have talked to me first," Sarah heard her mother saying.

"I didn't put up a fuss when you bought that bathing

72

suit," Mr. Gordon protested. "That was supposed to convince me, remember?"

"Ski boots are much more expensive than a bathing suit!"

"That's not the point. Besides, I didn't buy them for you yet. I just made a down payment, and an appointment for your fitting at the ski shop."

"It's not about the boots, Donald. I just don't want to go skiing. You're much better at it, and I'll be stuck on the beginners' slope while you're flying down the mountains. We won't see each other."

"What am I supposed to do with those skis downstairs?" Mr. Gordon said. "And what am I supposed to tell Eric at the ski store?"

"First of all, I couldn't make the appointment even if I wanted to, because I don't know when my case will be over. You can start by telling him I can't make it."

"Fine," said Mr. Gordon. "If I'd known you were going to be this stubborn—"

"*Me* stubborn?" Mrs. Gordon shot back.

Sarah pushed open the door and headed to the refrigerator. Her mother, who had been standing in front of it, moved aside. Mr. Gordon had perched himself on the counter near the sink; he eased himself to the floor.

"I have to get back to work," said Mr. Gordon, almost to himself. "I have a meeting with a parent."

As he left, Mrs. Gordon rinsed out her mug. She gave her daughter a sidelong glance. "How long were you outside listening?"

"Not long," Sarah mumbled.

"You look like the whole world is on your back. Is that what's bothering you: your father and me arguing?"

"Not really. I mean, partly..."

"We're having a disagreement; it's nothing terrible," Mrs. Gordon said with a smile. "We'll work it out somehow. Are Allison and Tasha upset about this?"

Sarah said she didn't think so. "It's not just you and Dad, it's just—"

"Did something happen between you and Dave?"

Sarah told her about the promise she had made to her girlfriends to avoid the boys until they stopped playing KAOS. She decided to leave out the details of the girls' kissing game. "I hate the boys' stupid killing game, but I can't tell Dave what to do," she added.

"That's right. What's fun for one person may not be for another—as your father and I keep trying to tell each other," said Mrs. Gordon with a sigh. "You have to tell him how you feel, and I'm glad you did. And if he decides to play after that, he has to understand your decision not to have any part of it."

"But I miss him," said Sarah.

"And he misses you," Mrs. Gordon assured her. "But he'll respect you more in the long run if you stand firm."

"You sound like Tasha, Mom," Sarah said with a grin.

After dinner, Sarah was just getting started on her

homework again when Allison called, "Sarah! Phone!"

"Hey, Sarah. It's Dave."

"Hi," she said after a slight pause.

"What's up?" he said in a friendly tone.

"Just doing my homework," Sarah replied.

"You want to do it together?"

"I can't," she said.

"It's because of the game, isn't it?" Dave said. "Why don't you lighten up?"

"I'm sorry, but that's the way I feel," said Sarah.

"Debby Barnes doesn't feel that way; I'll tell you that."

Sarah said nothing.

"Not the way she's been coming on to me lately," Dave continued. "She tried to kiss me today in the cafeteria, but I told her to cool it. I don't know what's going on." He paused and added, "Maybe I should have let her."

Although Sarah knew he was teasing and trying to break the tension between them, she couldn't help overreacting. "Is that how you're trying to get me to be nice to you?" she demanded angrily. "By threatening me with Debby?"

"Look, I'm just sick of the way you've been dogging me lately," he said.

"Then stop playing KAOS."

"No way," he said firmly. "It's fun, and I'm not hurting anybody. I don't care what you girls say. I'm not going to stop just because it upsets you!"

"Neither am I!"

"Fine!"

"Okay!" They each hung up without another word.

When Sarah turned to go back to her room, she saw Tasha standing at the doorway to her bedroom. "You okay?" she asked.

Sarah bit her lip. "I just had another fight with Dave. Look, Tasha—" She paused. "I'm thinking of dropping out of kissing KAOS. I made a fool of myself today trying to kiss Jimmy, and Debby's not playing by the rules. The whole thing is stupid. Let's just quit," she urged.

Tasha shook her head. "No way, cuz. I'm in this till the end. And so is Jennifer—you can't desert us."

Sarah sighed and headed for her room. Tasha and Jennifer would be really angry at her if she dropped out, and, even worse, Debby Barnes would think it was easy to push Sarah around.

As Sarah straightened up her room and got her things together for school the next day, she began to fume all over again over how easily Debby and Jimmy had made a fool of her today. I'm sick of being nice and playing by the rules all the time, Sarah thought. Watch out, Debby—and Dave, too—now it's all-out war.

Eleven

Tasha pounded on the bathroom door the next morning. "Let's go, cuz. The bus is coming, and Miss Essie isn't here to take us to Murphy if we miss it." Sarah emerged from the bathroom, and Tasha whistled. "Whoa, girl! You look hot!"

Sarah was wearing a pair of tight blue jeans with a shiny red blouse. The blouse was a little loose around the shoulders—a bra strap kept peeping through—but she kept it on. She had carefully applied lip gloss and brown powder on her face that made her dark complexion glow. "I'm ready," Sarah said with a grin. Her appearance was only part of today's plan.

The silky red blouse was a hit almost the minute Sarah took off her coat and stuffed it in her locker. Out of the corner of her eye, she could see Dave sneaking glances at her. She grinned with satisfaction. Now she needed to get Jimmy to notice her too.

As the day wore on, Sarah found herself getting

more and more comfortable in her new assertive role. It was Sarah who led her discussion group in English class that day. When a white boy in the class tried to interrupt her, she gave him a withering look, and said, "I'm not finished." He trailed off in midsentence.

And in the cafeteria when they were talking about who gave a better concert, Def Cru 4 or MC Whack, Sarah defended MC Whack even though she'd never really liked his music. The other girls were surprised at her position on the subject and how strongly she was arguing. Halfway through the period Debby, Linda, and Amanda approached their table. The girls were dressed in their pep squad uniforms.

"We're doing the yearbook picture after lunch," Debby explained. Suddenly she inhaled loudly. "Sarah, look at you! You're finally coming out of your shell," she said like a proud mother to her baby. Amanda giggled.

Sarah didn't reply.

"I heard you *almost* got Jimmy yesterday," Debby said innocently.

"Yes," said Sarah sweetly. "But he didn't push me into a muddy football field, thank goodness!"

Debby's smug expression froze on her face.

Kwame and José came up to the table before Debby could retort. "This table is for girls only," Debby said, giving them a stony look.

Sarah sighed loudly. She pulled out the chair she had been using to prop her feet. "Sit here, Kwame. You can sit next to Cindy, José."

Before Debby could say anything else, Sarah turned her attention to her friends and completely ignored Debby. Embarrassed, Debby spun on her heel and stormed off with the pep squad girls hurrying to keep up with her.

On her way to art class, Sarah spied Robert Thornton leaving his chemistry classroom. Impulsively she grabbed him by the shoulders and gave him a loud kiss on his cheek. As Robert shot her an astonished look, the magnitude of what she'd done began to sink in. Jennifer was going to be furious. Sarah had just kissed the boyfriend of one of her closest friends!

Jennifer arrived late to art class. She gave Sarah a dirty look as they took their sculptures down from the shelf. "That was really low, Sarah," Jennifer said furiously. "I thought we had an understanding not to go after one another's boyfriend. I thought we were on the same side."

Sarah began to dot her clay frog with drops of glaze. "Hey," she told Jennifer. "It's an open game. It's every girl for herself."

"I don't buy that," said Jennifer hotly. "Don't give me your stupid excuses either!" She stormed off and avoided Sarah for the rest of the class.

Sarah kept glancing at Jennifer. The hurt look on her face was more than Sarah could bear. She wanted to apologize, but she didn't know what to say. How could she explain that she'd somehow gotten carried away when she didn't understand it herself?

Twelve

Kwame unzipped his book bag and looked at his essay again. He had written four paragraphs on the role of blacks in the Civil War. He had rewritten the essay three times the night before and read it out loud to be sure it was as clear as he could make it. He wished he'd had more time, but what could he do?

He looked at the other students in the classroom and tried to judge his competition. As Mrs. Brewer had said, most of the science applicants were white. A girl named Christine who was in Kwame's history class was there, holding an application form identical to the one Kwame had completed. He smiled at her when she caught him looking. Christine's grades weren't as high as Kwame's, but their teacher always talked about her term papers with genuine admiration. She was black and female, and Kwame wondered if she would get more consideration because of that.

Mrs. Brewer walked in and smiled at them. With her

81

was a young white woman with a briefcase and red-framed glasses. The blue blazer she wore had a college crest on the lapel. She stood next to the teacher's desk in front of the room and waited for Mrs. Brewer to call the students to order.

"People, this is Ms. Hale; she's from the university internship program. I gave her a list of your names, and you are to hand in your application when you are called."

"First of all, let me make sure everyone who picked up an application is here today," said Ms. Hale. She read the names of the applicants for each internship. Kwame's heart beat faster and louder as she read through the list for African-American history. He heard Christine's name read, followed by other unfamiliar names. His name was the last to be called.

Ms. Hale looked at the apprehensive faces in the room and tried to reassure them. "I'm only here to take your applications and to get a very general impression of you. I won't be the only person evaluating your essays, so please try to relax a little. Some of you look very nervous."

The students laughed self-consciously. Ms. Hale started with the computer group, then the marine biology people, and finally the German students. Kwame checked his watch. If she didn't hurry, he would miss the late bus and have to call his father to pick him up. Kwame knew he was the last person on the list because Mrs. Brewer had tried to talk him out of applying. He glared at the counselor from the back of the room.

Then, with a shrug, he pulled out his books and decided to get a start on his homework while he waited.

When Kwame looked up again, the clock was approaching four, and Ms. Hale was still talking to Christine. He sensed a presence standing behind him and turned his head. It was Mrs. Brewer.

"I just want to tell you, Kwame, that I support your decision to apply," she began. "Maybe it wasn't right for me to try to talk you out of it, but I had your best interests at heart."

Kwame nodded politely, but he didn't like Mrs. Brewer's tone. She made it sound as if one day he would know better. He didn't know what to say. He looked at her silently and was glad when Ms. Hale finally called him forward.

The woman from the university took his application and glanced at the essay section. She nodded in approval and asked him about his interests. He beamed as he described how he read about and collected memorabilia from the Civil War. Gradually, Kwame relaxed and enjoyed the discussion.

"You must really like this stuff," Ms. Hale said.

"No," said Kwame. "Actually, I love it."

Ms. Hale smiled, and they talked well past the dismissal bell. He noted with pride that she had taken more time with him than with any of the other students. She apologized for taking so long, and even offered Kwame a lift if he would give her directions back to her hotel.

"Sure," said Kwame with a grin. They walked out to the parking lot and got into her rented car. "We're way behind schedule in our selection of interns," she confessed.

"When do we find out if we made it?" said Kwame.

"The director wants to narrow down the list of applicants by next week," said Ms. Hale.

Kwame felt his heart beating faster as she started up the car. He might know if he'd been selected by this time next week.

Thirteen

Mr. Schlesinger's first announcement on Monday morning surprised everyone. "The following members of the Murphy High community are to report to my office immediately after homeroom: Billy Turner, Dave Hunter, Steve Adams, Kwame Brown, Tyler McPeak, Robert Thornton, Derek Johnson...." He named the rest of the original KAOS players.

"How did he find out?" Billy whispered to the other boys as they waited outside his office.

"Probably from one of the sore losers." Tyler chuckled. He was already on his fifth victim.

The door opened and Mr. Schlesinger looked at the students standing outside. He was a tall, balding man with steel-rimmed glasses and a beard that formed a thin, furry line along his jaw. The boys filed into his office and stood fidgeting by the bookcase along the back wall.

"You know why you're here," he began. He paused to answer a knock on his door. Two custodians walked in, thick key rings clinking from their belt loops.

The students traded nervous looks, and a thin smile spread over the assistant principal's face. "If you have a water pistol in your book bag or your duffel bag, put it on my desk." Nobody moved. "*Now!*" he yelled. A few boys reluctantly unzipped their packs and turned in their guns. Mr. Schlesinger crossed their names off a list.

Billy was one of the boys who turned in his pistol. "Mr. Schlesinger, we weren't playing with the guns in school," he said.

"Don't lie to me, Billy. I got a note this morning telling me that you and some of the other KAOS players"— he looked at Steve and Dave —"were squirting the freshmen with high-pressure water guns. Some of those kids thought the guns were real! I won't have that." Dave and Steve started to protest, but Mr. Schlesinger raised his hands to quiet them. "Those students who didn't turn in a gun will wait in the office until the custodians search your lockers."

"Hey, man, you can't do that," said Sauk Weller. "We've got rights."

Mr. Schlesinger glared at Sauk, who was one of the biggest troublemakers at school. "A locker is not private property," he said. "I won't have water pistols or any other kind of guns at Murphy High. I'm surprised at you students. Such a childish game."

"Sir," said Dave, "we didn't play KAOS in school. That was a rule. Whoever told you that was lying."

"I doubt it," said Mr. Schlesinger. "My source

wouldn't lie."

"Well, then, they made a mistake," Dave insisted.

"That's enough, young man! You're in enough trouble as it is!" Mr. Schlesinger said vehemently. He swallowed hard. The students waited nervously.

Twenty minutes later, the custodians returned with three water pistols. They told Mr. Schlesinger the locker numbers they had come from, and Mr. Schlesinger checked them on his list. "We also found this in locker 216," said one custodian. He opened his hand and three marijuana cigarettes rolled onto the desk.

Kwame looked at Sauk out of the corner of his eye. Sauk hung his head. Mr. Schlesinger called him forward.

Billy Turner swore softly.

Sauk Weller's suspension was all over the school within the hour. Sarah, however, was more concerned about Dave and her other friends. She was surprised to see Dave waiting at her locker after her second class. He wasted no words.

"Is it true that you told Mr. Schlesinger about our game?"

"Of course not! Where did you get that?" she demanded.

"Somebody heard something," he said with a shrug. He looked relieved. "I didn't think you did."

"It's not true, Dave. I don't know where you got that story," she said. Sarah shook her head. "Are you and the others in a lot of trouble?"

"We're on probation," Dave replied.

"What does that mean?"

"It means if he catches us doing something else, we'll be in real trouble."

"Dave, believe me. I didn't tell him. You know I wouldn't do that," Sarah insisted.

"That's good enough for me," he said with a smile. He looked as though he wanted to say more, and Sarah hoped he would. He gave her a quick smile instead and then joined the crowd of students walking down the hall.

Sarah's mind was racing as she twirled the combination lock on her locker. Who could have started the rumor about her telling Mr. Schlesinger about the KAOS game? She didn't approve of the game, but she'd certainly never tell the administration about it.

As Sarah opened the locker, a folded notebook paper fluttered onto the floor.

"Dear Sarah" it read. "I hope you're happy. You got Jimmy and Tyler in a lot of trouble by telling on them. Did you tell Schlesinger about our game too?" It was signed by Debby. Sarah grimly folded the note and put it in her book bag.

"I heard a stupid rumor this morning," Cindy commented in the cafeteria that afternoon.

"Don't believe it," said Sarah. She showed her friend the note she had found in her locker. Cindy pursed her lips as she read it. "Debby probably tattled, then set you up."

"Don't worry," Sarah told her friend. "She won't get away with it."

When Jennifer and Robert Thornton sat down at the girls' table, Cindy's eyebrows shot up. "Are you out of the KAOS game, Robert?" she asked.

Robert looked at Cindy sheepishly. Before he could explain, Jennifer patted his shoulder.

"He's still in the game," she said coolly.

"But I thought we agreed—"

"I'm not down with that anymore," said Jennifer. "Besides, lots of people have been breaking the rules lately." She looked directly at Sarah

"I didn't break any rules," Sarah insisted. But her face turned red.

Kwame and Tasha arrived. They, too, asked Robert if he was no longer playing. Jennifer glared at Sarah again.

"Is it true you kissed Robert on Friday?" Tasha whispered to her cousin.

"Why not? He's one of the players, isn't he?" said Sarah.

"But Jennifer is one of us," said Tasha. "You should have gone after Tyler or Jimmy."

"I tried Jimmy, remember?" said Sarah, struggling to keep her voice down. "Look, cuz, I feel bad enough as it is, so don't rub it in."

By now the rest of the table was looking at the two cousins.

Cindy tried to change the subject. "Did you all hear about Sauk Weller's suspension?"

"Thanks to Sarah," Jennifer murmured. "If she hadn't told Schlesinger about the game, they wouldn't have searched his locker."

"I didn't tell him," snapped Sarah. "Debby's trying to get me in trouble. She thinks everyone will believe it because I'm usually such a goody-goody—and you fell for it."

Jennifer rolled her eyes. "You certainly haven't been very nice this week. I can't figure out what you're up to."

"You can think what you want," Sarah shot back.

Tasha was just sitting there, not saying a word. She's not even sticking up for me, Sarah thought. My own cousin thinks I tattled too.

Sarah grabbed her book bag and left the cafeteria. She made her way to the library, and sat in one of the carrels brooding.

Later in the period Cindy tapped her on the shoulder. "I thought you'd like to know. Debby, Linda, and Amanda showed up at our table a little while after you left."

Sarah shrugged. "Was she still telling everyone I told Mr. Schlesinger?"

Cindy nodded.

"I'll bet Jennifer believes her," said Sarah glumly. Cindy looked away. "Who else does?"

"Debby's just a troublemaker, " said Cindy quickly. "Forget about it."

Sarah touched her friend's arm. "Cindy, who else believes her? Kwame?"

90

Cindy shook her head.

"April? Tasha? She didn't say a word to me at lunch."

Cindy bit her lip. "Tasha was trying to stick up for you, but Debby has pretty convincing evidence."

Sarah stared at her friend. "And what's that evidence?"

"She's telling everyone she saw you talking to Mr. Schlesinger after school on Friday," Cindy replied softly. "She says you handed him a list of the KAOS players."

Fourteen

The activities lounge was technically open to all students, but an unwritten rule made it primarily a senior class hangout. Students were allowed to read, talk, and even eat at the long wooden tables in the middle of the room. The best seats, however, were near the windows overlooking the Murphy High playing fields. The upholstered chairs were comfortable enough to sleep in. They were usually occupied by seniors or "reserved" for them with book bags.

Tasha walked into the lounge that afternoon shortly before her study period was over. April had told her that Marc Halle usually spent his study period in the lounge, and she'd decided to make her move.

She found Marc sitting in one of the chairs by the window. He had propped his feet up on the low windowsill and sat in a comfortable slouch with a book in front of him.

"Let's see how good a kisser you are," Tasha murmured to herself as she walked toward him.

Marc kept glancing up from his book to watch the gym class that was playing soccer outside. When she was right behind him, Marc caught the scent of perfumed soap. He turned to see where the smell was coming from and was startled by how close Tasha was. He jerked his head back, and Tasha's kiss barely grazed his cheek.

When Marc saw who had been trying to kiss him, his eyes widened. Tasha looked great in her white denim skirt, wide metallic belt, and blue silk blouse. She took advantage of his surprise, leaned over and kissed him again. This time she didn't miss, and Marc didn't pull away.

What Linda had said about Marc's great kissing was true, Tasha realized. His lips were the warmest she had ever kissed and he took his time with it. What made it even more thrilling was that Marc was enjoying it too. Tasha felt her heart beating fast and she pulled back. Marc opened his eyes and gave her a grin that indicated he was interested in another round.

The bell rang and Tasha dashed out. She saw Kwame standing in the doorway with his mouth open.

"Kwame, it's not what you think," Tasha mumbled.

"What's not?" he said, unconvinced. "I thought you and Billy—"

"Please don't tell Billy," interrupted Tasha. "I had to kiss Marc, but I can't tell you why. Just don't tell."

Kwame nodded, still looking confused as Linda Plunkett walked past them. Tasha flashed a smile and said, "Hi, Linda," in her friendliest voice. Linda gave Tasha a suspicious look.

Marc almost ran past Linda, but she grabbed his shirt as he went by.

"What?" said Marc innocently.

"Did you just kiss Tasha Gordon?" Linda demanded.

"Huh?" said Marc. He swallowed. "No way!"

"Do you swear?" Linda said.

"I didn't kiss her. Ask anybody in the lounge," said Marc. "Tasha kissed me!"

Sarah decided she didn't want to face her friends at 18 Pine after school, so she decided to go to a slide show that was being hosted by the United Nations Club. It was called "America's Earliest People," and Sarah was interested in learning more about Native American culture.

She arrived at the slide show a few minutes late. On the screen was a slide of a Native American woman softening a piece of hide with her teeth. When Sarah got used to the darkness, she made out Kwame's shape near the front. Robert Thornton and Billy Turner sat in the back of the room. Robert kept making little comments under his breath that made Billy laugh into his hands.

Afterward they gathered near the stage, where the United Nations Club had set out two jugs of ice-cold cider, oatmeal cookies, and paper cups.

Billy had taken Michael Jay, a Navajo, aside to ask

him some questions about his people. Billy is a jock, but he doesn't fit the dumb athlete stereotype, Sarah thought. But then, neither does Dave.

When Sarah moved closer to hear what Michael was saying, she noticed that Billy was edging away from her. When she greeted him, he looked at her with suspicion. He thinks I told Schlesinger too, she thought. Sarah knew he was only reacting to the same rumor everyone else had heard, but it angered her anyway.

"Billy, I didn't tell anybody about KAOS," she said.

"Yeah, okay," said Billy. But he couldn't hide the skeptical look on his face. "Even if you did," he said, "no hard feelings, okay?"

That made Sarah feel even worse. You can't help being Miss Goody-Goody, Billy seemed to be saying. As she thought over the events of the day, something inside her gave way. If everyone—including my own cousin—is going to blame me, it might as well be for something I actually did.

"Tasha told me to give you something," she said. Billy raised a quizzical eyebrow and Sarah pounced on his mouth. She gave him the sweetest, most passionate kiss she could give to someone who wasn't Dave Hunter. But it was enough. She felt Billy resist at first, then relax and get into it for a fraction of a second before pushing her back.

"Next time," he said, catching his breath, "tell Tasha to give me the message herself!"

"I'm sorry, Billy," said Sarah meekly. "I guess I got carried away."

Sarah caught Kwame looking at the two of them with a shocked expression on his face. "Don't tell Dave what you saw," she said when she caught up with him. "I had to do it, but I can't tell you why. Just trust me, okay?"

Kwame nodded. It was the second time he had caught one of the Gordon cousins kissing someone besides her boyfriend. "Okay," he agreed. "But next time you or Tasha gets boy-crazy, look me up!"

As Sarah stood outside waiting for the late bus, she saw Billy heading toward the student parking lot. When Billy saw her, he smiled and waved her over.

"You want a ride home?" he asked, looking a little embarrassed.

Sarah shook her head. "You go ahead, Billy. I know it's out of your way."

"Suit yourself," said Billy with a shrug.

Sarah watched him leave, feeling a twinge of guilt about kissing him. If Tasha had kissed Dave, she reminded herself, her cousin probably wouldn't feel a thing. She sat on the low stone wall that encircled the flagpole and waved when Billy drove past. He rolled down the passenger window.

"Last chance, baby," he said with a grin.

She shook her head and he drove off. The buses pulled up to the school not long after, and Sarah stood up wearily. It had been a long day.

The students who'd been waiting inside for the bus came out of the building. Dave, who had been at basketball practice, walked up to Kwame.

"You want a ride, Kwame?" Dave said. He pointed to a teammate of his on the basketball team. "I'm taking him home and he lives near you."

"You know my motto: Never ask, but never turn down," said Kwame happily.

"How about you?" Dave said, turning to Sarah. He didn't look surprised when Sarah said no. "Come on, Sarah, you live across the street! I know this KAO thing bugs you, but don't be so uptight." Sarah gave him a cold look. "Look," he said, "just accept the ride. I promise we won't talk or get along!"

Sarah laughed in spite of herself and walked over to Dave's blue Dodge. They dropped off Kwame and the other boy first, then drove home in silence.

"How was the basketball game?" said Sarah.

"We won," said Dave. "Debby was there," he said after a pause.

"Did she . . . talk to you?" said Sarah.

"She tried to, but I was busy playing." He stole a look at Sarah. "What's with you and Debby? Sometimes you act like friends, and sometimes you're at each other's throat." He paused for a moment. "Sometimes I feel like I'm caught in the middle. I don't understand what's going on."

"I don't really know," said Sarah truthfully, wishing she could be honest with Dave.

He stopped in front of the Gordons'. Before Sarah opened her door, Dave tapped her on the shoulder. "Hey, Sarah. Let's treat ourselves to a nice date when this is all over."

"What did you have in mind?" said Sarah.

"We could go out to dinner, take a walk, maybe even go to one of your movies," said Dave, referring to the romantic adventure films she liked. He preferred a good horror film.

"I could go for that," said Sarah eagerly.

Dave gave her a grin that sent a current of electricity through her. When Sarah closed his car door, he peeped his horn lightly before turning into his driveway across the street.

Fifteen

Although Miss Essie's bags were leaning against the staircase, it was the smell of frying chicken that had told Sarah her grandmother was home.

"Miss Essie!" Sarah called out.

"That you, Sarah?" said Miss Essie, coming out of the kitchen. Her apron had batter on it, and her hands were dusted white with flour. She gave her granddaughter a quick hug.

"You just got back and they've got you working in the kitchen!" said Sarah.

Miss Essie laughed. "When I come home, that's a special occasion, and that calls for my fried chicken and vegetable dumplings for your cousin," she said.

Sarah followed Miss Essie into the kitchen and watched her turn the pieces of chicken that hissed in the hot oil. When they were golden brown, she lifted them out with a slotted metal spoon and laid them on a paper towel.

"How did the commercial go?" Sarah asked.

"The commercial was fine," Miss Essie said. "The coffee wasn't. But they must have liked the job I did." She sighed and pointed with her foot to a cardboard box near the refrigerator. It was a case of Mornin' coffee, compliments of the company.

Mr. Gordon walked into the kitchen in his favorite flannel shirt and a pair of faded cotton trousers. His eyes twinkled mischievously. "How are my two favorite ladies?" he said.

"Better not let my daughter-in-law hear you," said Miss Essie.

"Or Tasha," said Sarah.

"I know better than that," Mr. Gordon assured them.

"What are you up to?" said Miss Essie, eyeing her son. "And don't lie to me."

Mr. Gordon gave her a hurt look. "What makes you think I'm up to anything? But since you asked..." He left the kitchen and returned with two brightly colored envelopes.

"Plane tickets!" cried Sarah.

"Shhh! It's a surprise."

Sarah's eyes widened when she read the destination. "Cancún, Mexico! But Dad, I thought you wanted to go skiing."

"Some other time," he said.

"Mom's going to love it!" she said.

"All I can say is, it's about time, son," said Miss Essie, returning to her cooking.

After dinner Mr. Gordon made a big show of going

into the kitchen for dessert. He came back with a covered platter. When he raised the lid, Mrs. Gordon saw a little palm tree made from cucumber peels, and two dough figures playing with a radish beach ball.

"That's so cute!" cried Allison.

Mrs. Gordon gave her husband a bewildered look just as he produced the plane tickets from his shirt pocket and dropped one onto her plate.

"Oh, Donald!" Mrs. Gordon wailed. "Why didn't you tell me you'd changed your mind?"

"It was a surprise," Mr. Gordon replied in a puzzled tone. He put down the tray.

"Oh, Donald!" Mrs. Gordon repeated. She left the table and returned with her briefcase. She opened it and took out two tickets for Vail, Colorado. They looked at each other, dumbfounded.

Miss Essie chuckled first, but she struggled to keep quiet. Her efforts made Sarah giggle, and soon the whole table was laughing, especially Mr. and Mrs. Gordon. Sarah's mother finally caught her breath and wiped her eyes with her napkin. "That was a surprise, all right," she said.

"We'll take your tickets back tomorrow," offered Mr. Gordon generously.

"No," said Mrs. Gordon. "When I went to the travel agency, I saw some posters of Colorado and I got excited to go."

"Still," Mr. Gordon insisted, "you had your heart on the tropics all along. We can't let that red bathing suit go to waste."

"No, I mean it, Donald," said Mrs. Gordon.

"Here we go again!" said Miss Essie.

"We're going to Cancún whether you want to or not," said Mr. Gordon with a faint smile. "My tickets are nonrefundable."

"So are mine," said Mrs. Gordon. An awkward silence fell over the table.

"I don't believe this!" said Mr. Gordon. "You mean we both spent hard-earned money for these and now we can't return them?"

"Yes, but it happened, and there's nothing we can do to change it."

Mr. Gordon didn't reply. He paced back and forth for a moment. "We'll put an ad in the paper and sell the tickets that way. At least we can get some of our money back. Maybe someone at the office wants to go to Vail."

"We should try to sell the Cancún tickets," said Mrs. Gordon. "More people would be interested in that."

"We're going to Cancún, dear," he said, an edge creeping into his voice.

Mrs. Gordon drank from her water glass and said nothing. Sarah could tell she was getting angry.

Miss Essie went to the kitchen and took out the real dessert, fresh pineapple, but nobody was in the mood.

When Sarah and Tasha washed the dishes that evening, Tasha boasted about kissing Marc Halle again. "Wait till I get my lips on Tyler McPeak!" she said gleefully.

Sarah felt a pang of remorse. You're out of the

game, she wanted to say, but she couldn't bear to see her cousin's angry reaction.

"I'm going to track Tyler down just like I tracked down Marc," Tasha went on.

"I'll be right back," said Sarah. She went to the hall telephone upstairs and dialed the Turners'. I have to make sure Billy doesn't tell her, she thought anxiously.

No one she knew well, except for Kwame, had seen her kiss Billy—maybe Tasha would never find out.

When the answering machine clicked on at Billy's house, Sarah left an urgent message for Billy to call her.

But he never did.

Sixteen

The next morning as Billy was driving to school, he saw a large green army bag in the middle of the road. It blocked the street, and he couldn't get around it because a car was double-parked next to it. He got out of his car and pulled the heavy cloth bag to the side of the road. As he was returning to his car, he felt the high-pressure water gun drilling into his back.

"What the—" he started to say. Tyler McPeak stood there, grinning. He had a squirt gun in his hand. Billy cursed.

"You fell for my trap!" said Tyler, laughing as he opened the trunk of the double-parked car and threw the green bag into it. "I had to carry this bag in my trunk for two days before I got a shot at you. You're one tough dude to hit."

"Spare me, Tyler," Billy grumbled. He walked back to the car and took out a piece of paper with "Dave Hunter" written on it.

Tyler glanced at the name before shoving the piece of paper in his pocket. "I'm making a collection of these name slips," he told Billy. "I should have been a gangsta!"

In school that morning, Mr. Schlesinger announced over the PA system that the sophomores had tied the juniors in the canned food drive. Kwame's homeroom broke into a cheer. Ordinarily, he would have joined in their enthusiasm, but he had other things on his mind. He was still reeling from the letter he had received early that morning. The envelope from the internship program was ominously thin. He knew without opening it that it was bad news, because rejection notices always went out before acceptance letters. A college student had once told him that, and the internship was no exception. His full name had been typed onto a form letter:

"We were overwhelmed by the unusually high caliber of applicants for our summer programs. Arriving at a suitable number of interns proved to be an extremely difficult task. We regret we were not able to include all of the qualified applicants. . . ."

Kwame stopped reading there. His eye fell to the bottom of the page, where a note had been scribbled in blue ink:

"Kwame, I'm sorry about this. You were among the top students, but most of the applicants we accepted had participated in previous summer programs at the school, and preference was given to them. Who knows? Maybe one of the students will drop out. Catherine Hale."

The last sentence confused him until he read the rest of the letter, which informed him that he had been chosen as an alternate. The news didn't make him feel much better.

Mr. Schlesinger's next announcement caught his attention. "Congratulations are in order for the following student internship winners," he said. Kwame listened as Mr. Schlesinger read the names of four white boys he barely knew. Two had been accepted for the marine biology course, one for the computer course, and another for the German language internship. No one from Murphy had gotten the African-American history internship.

After homeroom Kwame ran to the main office. He made an appointment with the secretary to see Mrs. Brewer that afternoon. He wanted to know if she had found out anything from the black colleges. But he also harbored a suspicion that Mrs. Brewer had somehow hurt his chances for the internship. He wondered if Mrs. Brewer had tried to act in his "best interest" by telling Miss Hale not to accept him. It was a wild thought, but he wanted to make sure. If it turned out to be true, he vowed to make a huge fuss about it.

Christine, the girl from his class who had also applied, saw him in the hall and gave him a sympathetic smile. "Sorry about the internship," she said.

"Me too," Kwame said. "Maybe it'll happen next year for both of us."

In the cafeteria the school nurse had set up a display table as part of the school's Food Awareness Days. A video monitor showed a tape that discussed good eating habits. The machine rewound itself and played the short video over and over. "There it goes again," said Kwame wearily. The video was beginning to get on everyone's nerves.

As the tape began its peppy theme music, Kwame and José imitated the song with a forced cheerfulness.

"Stop!" said Tasha, holding her ears. "The real song is bad enough."

Billy took a seat next to Tasha at the cafeteria. "Well, I'm out. Tyler got me on my way to school this morning."

"Welcome back," said Tasha, giving him a kiss on the cheek.

When Sarah saw Billy sitting at their table, her heart began to beat faster. "Billy, are you out of the game?" she asked.

"Since this morning," he replied.

"Did you get my message?" said Sarah. Billy gave her a curious look. "The one I left in your locker," Sarah said, nodding slightly. But Billy clearly didn't know what she was talking about. Sarah's mouth began to feel dry.

"The old group is coming back," April announced. "Steve, Dave, and Robert are the only friends of ours still playing."

Sarah tried to pull Billy to one side, but he was

happy to be sitting with Tasha again. "What is it?" he said, getting the attention of the whole table.

"Nothing," said Sarah lightly.

"Heads up, cuz," Tasha said urgently. She pointed to the table where Dave, Steve, and Robert were sitting. Linda Plunkett was coming up behind Dave. Sarah watched helplessly as Linda reached over and...didn't kiss him! Instead Linda tapped his shoulder and whispered something in Dave's ear. Abruptly Dave stood up and walked over to Michael Jay.

With cold dread Sarah suddenly understood what Dave was asking him. She saw Michael nod slightly. Dave looked at Sarah and Billy. Sarah had never seen him look so angry.

"What was that all about?" April asked.

"We'll find out in a minute," said Billy. As Dave strode toward them, Billy looked down at Tasha and said, "By the way, Tasha. Thanks for yesterday's 'message.'"

"Billy!" Sarah cried.

"What message was that?" said Tasha.

"You know," said Billy with a grin. He winked at Sarah and turned to Tasha with a loud kissing noise.

Tasha froze for a moment, then looked at her cousin with hurt in her eyes. "You didn't, Sarah! How could you?"

Dave got to the table just then. He shoved Billy hard. "Yo, Billy, whassup?" he said in a tone Sarah had never heard before.

It took Billy only a second to spring out of his chair

111

and fend off the next shove. "What are you doing?" he shouted.

Dave shoved him again. The attention of everybody in the cafeteria was fixed on the two friends, who were shoving each other harder and harder.

"Why are you moving in on Sarah?" Dave demanded.

"You're bugging out, man," said Billy. "I didn't do anything to her."

Sarah was horrified at the spectacle that followed.

Dave and Billy were fairly evenly matched. What Billy lacked in height, he made up for in bulk. They rolled on the floor, each trying to pin the other. Then a woodshop teacher, who weighed close to three hundred pounds, broke through the crowd. He simply sat down and straddled the two boys. Exhausted and gasping for air, the two boys relaxed their holds on each other. Finally the teacher stood up and yanked them to their feet.

"This is all your fault, Sarah," Tasha snarled. "Why did you kiss Billy?"

"Because you didn't believe me when I said I wasn't the one who told about KAOS!" Sarah shouted back, her voice breaking as she blinked back the tears. "I'm sick of everyone considering me a goody-goody! Haven't you even noticed that I've been trying to act differently?"

"Stop it, both of you!" said José, moving between the two girls.

Sarah suddenly felt a hand on her shoulder. Another

112

monitor put one hand on Tasha's shoulder and took Sarah firmly by the arm. "You two, come with me," he said.

From the back of the crowd, Debby, Linda, and Amanda looked on, amused. "There goes the 18 Pine St. gang," said Debby with a giggle. "Boy, Dave really went crazy."

"He must really like Sarah," said Amanda, almost to herself.

Debby looked at her friend with annoyance. "Yeah that's true love, all right," she said sarcastically. "But look what it got him."